MAEVE & THE WOLF

ANNA ROMER

For Russell

"Midway along the journey
of our life I woke to find myself
in a dark wood, for I had wandered
off from the straight path."
—Dante Alighieri, *Inferno*

1

MAEVE

THE FOREST SEEMED ABRUPTLY HUSHED, the tall trees rustling softly in the stillness as I slowed my pace on the narrow hiking trail. Bright afternoon sunbeams pierced the thick canopy of leaves, flickering a mosaic of light on the forest floor around me. Goosebumps rose on my arms as I looked back over my shoulder.

I couldn't see him, but I felt his presence.

Moving quietly, his tread silent as shadows. Following my scent, or maybe just curious about why I was here. A creature of the night, a wild thing. A dangerous thing. But as long as I stayed on the track, he couldn't hurt me.

At least, that's what I told myself as I adjusted my backpack, clutching the small bouquet of native wildflowers closer to my chest, walking deeper into the forest along the winding trail.

The grasses and ferns became sparser as the trees grew thicker, their branches knitting together to block out the sun. My sneakers crunched over a carpet of decaying leaves and brittle twigs, the path inclining steadily uphill. A lone butterfly flitted near my face, its wings a yellow blur as it zoomed upwards into the bright blue above.

"I'm doing this for you, Alec," I whispered. "And for me."

For two years, I had stayed away from this place. But Dr Palmer said it was time—time to face the memories, to make peace with what happened. I couldn't keep living half a life, couldn't keep letting the nightmares win.

I crouched to pick up a banksia seedpod, slipping it into my collection bag. Old habits. Even on this pilgrimage, I couldn't help myself. Seeds had always been my passion, my connection to life and renewal. At least they had until...

"Don't go there, Mae."

My therapist would be proud of me. Venturing out alone, living my life. Acting brave. Ignoring the suspicion that someone—or some*thing*—was following me. After two years, I had finally shaken off my nightmares and started making progress. Getting back to what I loved. What I needed. Hiking in the bush. Communing with nature.

Finding the person I'd been before.

Before...

Leave it alone, Maeve. It belongs in the past now.

Like so much of my life. But that was about to change. Collecting seeds from rare plants had once been the centre of my world. And with my government permit renewed, I could roam freely through the state forest again, gathering samples while my soul revived itself. Yes, there were moments when my memories howled at me and made my heart race, but I did my best to ignore them.

I shivered despite the warm air.

My best friend Kitty said I was crazy to return here. *Aren't you scared of the forest now, Maeve? After what happened to Alec?*

I clutched the bouquet tighter.

"We're the scary ones, Kit. Us humans. Cutting down old-growth trees. Bulldozing habitat." I trailed my gaze along the edge of the shadowy undergrowth. "Shooting the wild dogs who are only trying to survive out here, which can't be easy."

You should be glad they're culling the dogs, after what the mongrels did. How do you know there's not one stalking you right now?

I stopped walking.

"There's nothing here," I said, hating how my voice wavered. "Just me and the trees and the memories I need to face."

Yeah, the trees. I glanced over my shoulder. Why did it feel like they were watching me? With their twisted branches cutting off the sky and moss gripping their rough bark, shadows twitching at their feet.

"Okay, Maeve. Breathe."

I gulped and kept going. According to the map, I was getting close to the spot. The clearing where it happened. Where Alec's screams had torn through the night. Where I'd stood frozen, too paralysed by terror to help him as the creature attacked.

I had always dreamed of being a wild girl—one of those free spirits who shook out her hair and danced in the rain or sped along the river road on her gleaming trail bike, never caring what people thought. The sort of girl Nan used to warn me about. *Girls who stray from the path come to a bad end, Maeve. Don't let yourself become one of them, you hear?*

I'd taken Nan's words to heart and moulded myself into someone who never strayed, or even questioned what lay beyond the path. But lately, while packaging seeds for my nursery, gazing up at the stars, or swamped by the loneliness of my cottage on the edge of town, I found myself wondering.

What was out there? And was it really so bad—?

A ray of light cut through the gloom, picking out a bright blue orchid. The plant was well off the track and deeper in the forest. I hesitated, the flowers in one hand, my collection bag in the other. The clearing where Alec died was just ahead, but that orchid...

"Maybe a quick detour," I whispered, stepping off the path. "Just for a moment."

I made my way through the undergrowth, drawn by the vibrant blue petals, each step taking me further from the safety of the trail. Beside the orchid sat a withered clump that made my pulse fly—a second plant nodding under the weight of a large ripe seedpod.

"You perfect little sweetheart," I breathed, moving toward the pod. "You're coming home with me!" Three more steps and I'd reach it, dry leaves crackling under my boots. Two more steps—

I jerked to a stop as a blur of silver-grey exploded from the shadows.

A massive wolf-like creature launched itself at me, jaws open, eyes blazing. I screamed, stumbling backward as it landed just in front of me, hackles raised, teeth bared in a savage snarl.

The flowers tumbled from my grip as I fell, scattering across the forest floor. The wolf loomed over me, its growl vibrating through the air, sending waves of terror through my body.

I scrambled backwards, my skin turning hot. Then ice cold.

It's happening again, only this time it's happening to me.

The big dog advanced, each step deliberate, its massive paws crushing the fallen flowers, its snowy muzzle twitching. Its eyes —pale grey-green, flashing silver in the dappled sun—never left mine, fierce and savage and somehow ... urgent.

I couldn't move. Couldn't breathe. My muscles turned to stone as the creature edged closer, its musky scent over-whelming my senses.

You need to run, Maeve. Run as fast as you can and don't look back.

With a choked sob, I lurched to my feet and bolted toward the path, heart thundering, lungs burning. I ran blindly, branches whipping my face, roots catching at my feet as I crashed through the undergrowth, desperate to reach the path.

A loud, metallic snap came from behind me and something let out a howl that seemed to shake the forest. The sound triggered a memory I'd fought so hard to bury—

Alec is screaming in the darkness. Our campfire just embers, the night forest silent around us, except for his cries and the savage snarls. The scent of damp earth and decaying leaves mixing with a strong animal odour. Dog. Wolf. Then comes the metallic stench of blood, thick and sticky as it splatters onto my arm, burning with each drop as Alec keeps screaming, and me standing frozen, unable to move or do anything to help him.

I gasped, the flashback shattering as I stumbled onto the trail.

I didn't look back. Didn't stop to collect my scattered things or to lay the flowers at Alec's spot. All I wanted was to escape, to flee back to my car, back to safety. *As long as you keep to the path, nothing can hurt you.*

I had strayed, just for a moment. And now I knew with terrifying certainty—the wolves were still out here. The same creatures that had torn my husband apart were hunting these woods. Hunting me.

2

THE WOLF

I BOUNDED SILENTLY behind the human female, paws barely disturbing the forest floor. Hunger clawed at my insides. Two days since my last kill—a scrawny rabbit that barely filled the hollow in my belly. But it wasn't food that drew me to her.

Her scent was ... everything. Rich. Complex. Layered like forest soil after rain. Beneath the sharp tang of her fear lay something else—something that made my nose twitch and my heart quicken. Something familiar.

I kept to the shadows between trees.

Years ago, I made a mistake. Let my guard down. Humans were untouchable, that was law. But my error led them to our den-places, the dark corners where my kind had always been safe. Now the pack was scattered, driven to the ancient woods where trees blocked the sun and prey ran thin.

I hadn't meant to follow this one. Was tracking a fox when her scent cut across my path—warm skin, crushed wildflowers, and that strange metal humans carry. But beneath it all, a familiar note I couldn't place.

Her breathing changed when she sensed me—quick, shallow. Heart drumming so loud I heard it from twenty paces back. A tiny gasp escaped her when my shadow flickered between trunks.

Then—she veered suddenly from the path, drawn by a flash of blue. A flower.

Something else caught my attention. The faintest whiff of metal and oil. My hackles rose instantly.

Trap.

There, beneath the fallen leaves where she was heading. Human hunters had laid their cruel metal teeth, waiting to snap closed on any creature that crossed their path.

She was unaware. Walking straight towards it.

I didn't understand the surge of panic that flooded my veins. She was human—the enemy. The ones who drove us from our territories, who hunted my kind. Yet I couldn't let her step into that trap. The thought of those metal teeth closing on her fragile flesh made my heart race with fear.

Without thinking, I burst from the undergrowth. Lunged towards her, teeth bared, a warning growl tearing from my throat. Had to frighten her. Had to make her stop, turn back.

Her eyes widened, terror flooding her scent. She fell backward, away from where the trap lay hidden. Good. Safe. But the fear in her eyes—it twisted something inside me. Made me want to press close, show her I meant no harm.

Impossible. I was what humans feared in the darkness. They were what I feared, too.

She scrambled away, flowers scattered across the forest floor. Her fear-scent sharp and overwhelming. I watched her flee back to the safety of the path. Only when she was gone did I turn to leave. My paw caught the edge of a twig—and the trap slammed shut.

PAIN.

Metal teeth clamped around my foreleg, biting through fur,

through flesh, through bone. A sound ripped from my throat—half-howl, half-scream. My body convulsed, twisting against the trap. Blood—hot, thick, mine—pulsed between the metal jaws, dripped to the forest floor. The rich copper scent of it filled my nostrils.

My teeth snapped uselessly at the unyielding trap. Each movement sent fresh agony shooting up my leg. I knew this pain. Had seen creatures caught this way before. Had heard their cries fade to whimpers as the light left their eyes.

I knew what followed.

Humans with their guns that spat death. Humans who laughed while they skinned my kind for their pelts.

I dragged myself in a circle, metal chain rattling behind me. My breath came in hot, ragged pants. My vision grew cloudy. I rolled my eyes upwards, but the moon could not help me while the dying sun still shone. I threw myself backward, muscles straining, bone grinding against metal.

Fight. Must fight.

But deep inside, where the wild met the knowing, I understood.

Was this how it ended?

And yet—I couldn't regret it. The female was safe. The human with the familiar scent had escaped the trap that now held me. It made no sense that I cared. No sense at all.

But as darkness crept into the edges of my vision, her scent lingered in my memory. Something about her ... something I needed to understand before the end came.

3

MAEVE

I RAN BACK along the hiking trail until my lungs burned and my legs trembled, the forest a blur around me. Only when I reached my car did I stop, collapsing against the door, gasping for breath.

"Never again," I promised, hands shaking as I fumbled with my keys. "Never again."

Yet even as I sped away, tyres spitting gravel behind me on the forest road, something stirred inside me. As my heart rate slowed, a small, detached part of me wondered about the wolf's grey-green eyes. They hadn't looked mindlessly savage like the ones in my nightmares.

They had looked ... *knowing*.

Almost human.

I shuddered, glad when I emerged onto the bitumen road that led back to town. Soon the forest thinned out, and the hiking trail—and the monster lurking there—began to seem like a distant nightmare.

I dug around in my glovebox and grabbed my emergency

chocolate stash. The wrapper crinkled as I peeled it away and demolished the sweet treat in a few bites.

Wolves had been in Riverwood for as long as I could remember. As a child, I'd heard stories about them. And warnings. *If you must go into the forest, keep on the path. Wolves are deadly but also shy. They won't come for you—unless you stray into their domain.*

No other area in Australia had a wolf problem—they just didn't exist here in the wild. Except for Riverwood. Nan said that forty years ago, a deer eradication program backfired, and an introduced pack escaped into the forest. As far as the government was concerned, out of sight was out of mind. But over the years there'd been sightings.

And killings.

Calves. Sheep. Foals. If someone went missing, the locals blamed the wolves. No matter if that person turned up later, the legends only seemed to grow. After what happened to Alec, the hunters grabbed their rifles and went looking, culling plenty of feral dogs and dingoes along the way. The wolves were hated here, with good reason—they were savage, beastly things that deserved everything they got—

"Stop it!" I unclamped my stiff fingers from the wheel. "I'm spooked enough, okay?"

I drove to my native plant nursery on the south side of town. It's name—Nan's Wild Posy—was a play on my nan's name, Posy. Her legal career had kept her away from gardening most of her adult life, but now in retirement, she devoted all her time to her plants. When I opened my nursery, it seemed a no-brainer to name it after her.

I went straight to the fridge at the rear of the shop in search of comfort food. I found some of Nan's cake left over from lunch and stood with the fridge door open, scarfing it down, the sugar hit reviving me.

"Maeve?" Kitty barged in, her arms overflowing with seed trays. She wasn't scheduled to work today, but she often came in to pot up plants for her property on the outskirts of town. "I thought you'd gone to Nan's?"

"Not yet." I gestured at the fridge. "Just ... getting a snack."

"You look terrible. All pasty and weak."

"Yeah, thanks."

She frowned, setting aside the trays. "You've got leaves in your hair. And is that a graze on your face? Please tell me you didn't—"

I dusted cake crumbs off my fingers and ran them through my tangled hair, elbowing my cheek where I'd bounced off a tree. Unable to meet her eyes.

"You bloody fool," she said gently, coming over to give me an awkward one-armed hug. "Next time you go into the forest, let me know and I'll come with you."

"Sure." I untangled myself and collected the plants I'd set aside for Nan, then retrieved my bag and keys. "I'll tell Nan you said hello."

Kitty nodded and trailed after me, thoughtful. "You know, Mae. What happened to Alec wasn't your fault. It was tragic, of course. But you couldn't have saved him."

"I know."

"I'm just glad it wasn't you."

"Is that meant to make me feel better?"

"Yeah." She raised her brows at me. "Doesn't it?"

"I guess—in a bitter and twisted kind of way."

"Then quit blaming yourself, okay?"

I stopped and slowly turned. Kitty was older than me, in her forties and gorgeous with her mane of pale gold hair and Nordic features, so like Nan's. She was my best friend and foster sister, and the person I trusted most in the world—next to Nan. Yet I hadn't told her everything about Alec and what happened that night in the forest. Some things were too shameful to share, even with her.

"I'm getting there, Kit. I promise."

Her smile wasn't quite convincing, but she perked up suddenly. "Hey, let's go to the Glade on Saturday. It'll be fun. You can practice getting back into the swing of things."

"Um. I don't know."

"Aww, go on. Please?"

I blew out a breath. "We'll see."

As I crossed the car park, she called out to me.

"Don't forget your togs, we'll go for a swim!"

I waved feebly back and unlocked my car, dropping my keys as I climbed in. I wasn't sure how I felt about her plan. Riverwood had only one social hub in summer, and that was the sandy picnic area that everyone called the Glade. The whole town would be there, sunbaking and swimming in the river. Grilling their sausages and steaks, and hanging out with their families.

Including the Lambs.

I started up the car, muttering under my breath.

"Maybe I'll come down with something nasty on Friday night. Toothache. A stomach bug. A severe case of avoiding the in-laws-itis."

Sounded like a plan.

I saw Derek Lamb too much as it was. After Alec died, his older brother took a sudden interest in me. Dropping by the shop unannounced, turning up to help with odd jobs. It might have been sweet—if only he didn't creep me out so much. Kitty had hinted that Derek was a catch, pushing me to move on and give him a chance. But she didn't know what I knew about the Lamb family.

And I had no intention of ever telling her.

4

MAEVE

Nan lived on the leafy north side of town, a forty-minute drive from my plant nursery. Posy Winters was not my real grandmother. She'd taken me in as an eight-year-old foster child after her adult daughter passed away, and had never allowed me to leave. Not that I ever wanted to. She was my mum, dad, nanna and grandad all rolled into one. My absolute hero.

"Ah, Nan."

Once, I could have told her anything. Maybe even all about the Lambs. About Alec. But Nan had troubles of her own these days, and I was doing my best to be strong for her.

Just as she'd always been strong for me.

I buzzed down the windows, letting the cool evening air wash over me.

Love is a curse, Nan used to say. *It always starts as a fairy-tale, but the minute you drop your guard, the monsters come out to play, stomping on your dreams and crushing your chance at a happy ever after.*

"I should have listened, Nan."

The first time she said love was a curse, I laughed.

Not just laughed—I'd tossed back my head and let out a full-on hoot. I was immune to curses back then—or so I thought. Because how could I be cursed when Alec Lamb had chosen me? The shy, quiet girl who loved to read and never said boo. The girl with unruly auburn hair and amber eyes who found it hard to hold anyone's gaze for more than a few seconds? The girl so scared of monsters and shadows and getting pregnant that she never once strayed off the path?

And yet somehow, Alec *had* chosen me.

Alec freaking Lamb. With his chiselled jaw and lush lips, and eyes that seemed to see beyond my mousiness to the kitten lying dormant beneath. Alec was Riverwood's golden boy. The rugged logger's son who made every girl in Riverwood High swoon. I was the last person he should have fallen for. Me, the quiet bookworm, always hiding behind a stack of books in the library, drawing cats. Or writing letters to the Forestry Commission about the old-growth trees we should be saving.

Yet Alec had noticed, and no one was more shocked than I was. Straight after high school we got married, and everyone said how perfect we were together. A fairytale couple, they called us. Which always secretly astounded me, considering how different we were. Big strong Alec with his flannel shirt and bulging biceps, his easy charm. And shy, bookish Maeve, who mostly kept to herself. Yet everyone predicted we'd last forever. And in the beginning, even I believed we stood a chance.

But the minute you let down your guard...

I sighed, searching my tongue along my bottom lip for cake crumbs.

"You were right all along, Nan. Love is definitely a curse."

Two years ago, we buried Alec—or what remained of him —in the Lamb family plot at Riverwood Cemetery. Along with him, I had buried my certainty. My belief in myself, my courage. Sure, I'd inherited his successful sawmill business and our renovated cottage, along with his substantial bank account. But nothing could fill the void of uncertainty his death had left behind. As if he'd taken a chunk of my soul into the grave with him.

I slowed the car, squinting into the roadside trees.

This was usually the darkest stretch before Nan's. Towering ironbark trees lined the roadside, their leafy canopies blotting out the moonlight. On my right, the old sawmill emerged from the shadows, its weathered walls eerie as my headlights swept over it.

Was that firelight flickering behind it?

It was summer, the worst time for fires. Too close to the sawmill for comfort. My sawmill. And the thousand hectares of land it sat on—land I privately dreamed of turning into a wildlife haven. One day. As I pulled off the road into the mill parking lot, the rumble of drunken shouts and laughter drifted through my open window.

My heart sank. "Derek."

I'd know that gruff laugh anywhere. Foreman of the sawmill, Derek Lamb was probably the scariest person I'd ever had the misfortune to meet. He was tall and powerfully built like Alec, though lacking his brother's boyish charm and talent for flirting. He was the fighter, the family protector. He'd taken Alec's death hard, and two years ago had made it his mission to punish the world for his loss.

Slipping out of the car, I crept over to the corrugated building that housed the mill. Out back, in a bare clearing, a blazing bonfire illuminated a group of men. They were standing around a river red gum tree, where a large dog strained against the rope tethering it to the trunk. The men were hurling beer cans and laughing as the dog bared its teeth and growled at them.

Leaning around the edge of the building, I frowned.

Derek Lamb stood head and shoulders over the others, the firelight casting him into shadow. He said something and the other men laughed, then he picked up a stone and launched it at the dog. When it struck the animal's face, it yelped in pain.

I inched forward for a better look.

The dog was huge and shaggy, its pelt matted with wet black stains. Blood. Poor thing, I felt sick for it. It looked so powerful, like an oversized shepherd, but its ribcage quivered as it panted in fear.

Why do you care, Maeve? One of those wild dogs mauled Alec, you should be glad it's suffering.

But I wasn't glad. Not even close. My heart ached like a pulled tooth. I knew how it felt to be trapped. To crave freedom. To lie in bed at night, staring at the ceiling, wondering how I'd get through another day—

A yelp jolted me back. Someone had thrown a stone, leaving a gash on the dog's ear. Derek raised his shotgun, firing a shot into the dirt beside the dog. The poor creature howled, twisting against the rope as it tried to wrench free.

The sound snapped something inside me.

I broke from the shadows and marched towards the group of jeering men, my legs wobbling under me, my damp fingers curled into fists.

5

———————

MAEVE

"WHAT THE HELL ARE YOU DOING?" My voice quivered in the night air. "I know you want to cull the dogs, Derek. But this is just cruel!"

Derek turned to face me, lowering his weapon.

The sight of him always gave me a jolt. He was so like his brother, only older and rawer. A big hulk of a man with intense eyes and a mocking smile.

"Stay out of it, Mae."

"Why don't you euthanise it humanely? Or let it go. Alec's gone. Killing more dogs won't bring him back."

The other men murmured, shuffling closer. One of them, Reg Garrett, who'd thrown the last stone, shouldered his rifle and sneered.

"Go home, Maeve. You don't belong out here. Leave us men to our business."

Ignoring him, I turned towards the dog. My breath caught. God, the sheer size of it. Must be part Bull Arab though it looked pure shepherd. Larger than any I'd seen before. Shaggier, too. Its snowy muzzle long and sharp, almost like a true wolf. A male, and under other circumstances it would have been magnificent.

I frowned, inching forward.

It seemed familiar. Despite the matted fur, there was no mistaking its long limbs in the flickering firelight—and the distinctive white muzzle. Just as I'd sensed its presence earlier in the forest, I sensed it again now. It was the same dog who'd tracked me along the hiking trail this afternoon.

A wolf.

My shoulders tightened as the breath left my lungs. Did it remember me? Remember how it tracked me and then sprang from the shadows, growling. It could have easily caught me, too … only it hadn't.

It whined, pawing the dirt. Not so fierce now, with its matted coat and mangled front paw. Not so scary. Crouched as he was, he seemed almost submissive.

"Hey," I breathed, stepping closer. His ears pricked at my voice, his pale eyes fixing suddenly to mine. "Good boy."

I approached cautiously, the men laughing and jeering behind me. I could smell the animal's blood now, sharp and sour in the night air. He growled and bared his teeth, his white muzzle flecked with foam, his eyes wary. Then his nostrils twitched and a stillness came over him as he settled onto the ground, looking up at me.

"You're a good boy, aren't you? You don't deserve this."

My fingers neared his muzzle and he sniffed again, the fear in his eyes softening. But then Derek strode up behind me, gripping my arm roughly and dragging me backwards away from the dog.

"What are you playing at, Mae? Trying to get yourself torn to bits like Alec?"

"Let me go!" I wrenched my arm free and glared up at him. "Stop tormenting the poor thing. Set him free, Derek."

"To kill again?" He shook his head and glared at the dog over my shoulder. "Not going to happen. That bloody thing is a killer. Look at the size of it. We saw it at Garrett's place, stalking his lambs. If we let it go, it'll be back there tomorrow slaughtering more. Is that what you want?"

"If Garrett's so worried, he should bring his lambs in at night."

Derek sucked on his lower lip, then grinned. "In where—to his bedroom?" The guys behind him smirked, and he shook his head. "That's not how it works, and you know it. Anyway." He leaned closer, his gaze dropping to my mouth, crawling over me a little before finding my eyes again. "Don't you want revenge?"

My legs trembled as I squared myself to meet his gaze, hating the way my voice wavered. "What you're doing isn't revenge, it's cruelty. I should report you all to the RSPCA."

Derek swayed closer, his shadow engulfing me, a half-smile teasing his lips. He was enjoying this. I could see it in his eyes.

"No need to get hysterical, Mae. Let us deal with it our way. Just turn around and scoot back to your car. It's late and you look terrible, by the way. You're all hollow in the face and pale. Shaking like a leaf."

"Please let the dog go."

"No."

"But—"

"We're doing this for Alec. The town's not safe with all these wild mongrels roaming free. These wolves deserve to be killed. If you wanna stay around and watch us do it, fine. If not, then go home."

A rifle clicked behind me. Reg Garrett strutted forward, aiming at the dog, squinting along the barrel. "Sure you can handle the heat, Mae?"

When Alec owned the mill, they'd never spoken to him this way. Never treated him with such insolence. Alec had swaggered around like king of the hill, lording it over all of them. And now that his brother was king, they did whatever he said, ignoring me.

I gazed around at the group. "I own this mill, remember? I could fire you all."

Derek's lips twisted in a silent snarl. Losing the mill to an outsider like me was still a sore spot for the Lambs, Derek most of all. He shifted closer till we were almost touching.

"You won't be firing anyone, Mae. You'd only have to replace us with contractors from out of town, and no one wants that. They're not bad blokes. They have families to feed, and they work hard. Sacking them would do you more harm than good."

His eyes narrowed as his gaze went to my lips again, and he touched his tongue to the corner of his mouth.

Bastard. He wasn't just enjoying this. He was getting off on it. He had adored his younger brother, but the whole ten years I'd been married to Alec, I had sensed friction between them whenever I was around. I never understood what a man like Derek would see in a quiet mousy bookworm, but there it was.

I broke away from him suddenly and lurched towards the dog. The animal snarled and strained on the rope at my approach, his ears flattening. But I bypassed him and went to the tree, tugging on the knotted rope, my fingers slick with sweat.

"Run," I said under my breath. The dog's ears pricked up, and he whined. The knot slithered apart and the rope slackened, falling free. "Run for your life and don't look back!"

He sped across the open ground towards the trees, the rope trailing after him. Derek and another of the men cocked their rifles and shot a few rounds, but the dog vanished into the shadowy forest.

I turned to Derek, trembling so hard I could barely stand.

My brother-in-law glowered at me. He wouldn't crack, not with the men around, but fury radiated off his broad shoulders, off the tight muscles in his neck.

He strode over and wrenched me up against him.

"Happy now, little Mae-Mae?"

My lip came up in a sneer as I pushed against him, trying to shove free.

"Don't call me that."

"That injured dog won't run far. We'll get him tomorrow."

I struggled against his grip. "Alec wouldn't have wanted this, you know. He might have been a reckless drunk, but he wasn't cruel. Not like this."

Derek cocked his head as if puzzled, but then he let me go and smiled. "My brother had his moments, Mae. You of all people should know that."

I rubbed my arms. There'd be bruises tomorrow.

"You're just peeved because he was the better man."

Derek reached for me suddenly and grasped the back of my head with his big hand, drawing my face close to his.

"Alec's not here to protect you now, sweetie. That's why you need me. And I guarantee the day will come when you'll beg me to eat you up like the big bad wolf I am."

"Get off me, you creep!"

I broke out of his grip, but then just stood there, trembling. Fighting tears as I summoned the energy to walk back to my car.

Derek smiled, and there was a sudden tenderness in his expression I'd never seen before.

"Go on, Mae." He spoke almost fondly, sounding like Alec. "Go home now. We'll talk about this later."

He gave me a light shove and maybe it was shock, or what little fight I had left draining away, but I started walking stiffly back to my car, tears clinging to my lashes.

I should never have stopped tonight. It was too horrible.

But at least the dog was free. For now. I could still see its beautiful, bloodied pelt and haunted eyes. And the way it had gentled at the sound of my voice.

"I hope you get away," I whispered, dashing tears off my face. "I hope you run as fast as you can away from Riverwood and never come back."

6

THE WOLF

I RACED through the pitch-black forest, my hind leg throbbing, my broken ribs creaking with each breath. Blood wept from the bullet hole in my flank, hot and sticky as it soaked my fur. The strangling rope that had bitten into my flesh was gone now, caught on a branch that had nearly taken my head off.

But I was free.

Thanks to the little human female. The same little one I'd frightened away from the trap today. And despite the hellish aftermath, I was still glad.

I panted hard, each breath drawing in the metallic tang of my blood. It burned against my hide as it flowed in a hot trickle, matting my coat. The primal instinct to stop—to lick the blood from my wounds and let my saliva mend the torn flesh—clawed at my mind. I ignored it. Instead, I raced toward the setting moon, following its mesmerising light as it sank in the northwest.

Follow the moon, urged my heart. *Follow its shimmering trail*, whispered my blood. *It will lead you home.*

As I ran, the female's voice drifted back to me, calm and gentle despite the acid fear that had radiated off her skin. Despite her trembling. She was not like the others. Not like the males. They were all yells and sharp edges, their deadly energy raising my hackles, their rope cutting into my neck as I twisted to break free. The female was different. Soft, like the rabbits I loved to catch and feast on. Like the baby lambs I crunched between my powerful jaws, tearing the flesh from their bones, drenching my mouth with blood and sweetness.

I didn't want to feast on the female.

Not in that way.

I didn't want to tear her flesh from her bones and lap her blood. Rather, I wanted to—

Bright lights speared through the darkness at the edge of the forest, startling me. Lights meant danger. They meant humans were nearby. Humans armed with guns and the sharp things they used to cut and kill. The lights danced at the periphery of my vision as I ran. They seemed to call out to me.

Run ... Run for your life and don't look back!

I changed direction, racing now towards the spears of light. As I approached the road that snaked along the forest edge, the purr of a car motor reached my ears. I thought of the female again. She had untied the rope and set me free. The males would have killed me. I had sensed their intent in the sharp reek of their body odour and in the harsh way their voices barked back and forth to each other.

But the female.

She had saved me.

Set me free, bringing the anger of the largest male onto herself. Not just anger but the mating fever, as if the large male wanted to possess her, cower her. Mount and dominate her. Was the big male planning to kill her?

I growled, veering alongside the road now.

As the car approached, I loped beside it, easily keeping up despite my injuries. Staying hidden in the trees as I raced the vehicle like a pup racing a rabbit.

I was panting hard. The wound in my flank burned, and a froth of saliva flicked off my tongue as I ran. Every bone in my body screamed at me to change direction, but the urge to chase the vehicle was stronger. Why was I being reckless?

The female.

I slowed, pricking my ears and lifting my nose to the air. Tiny tremors coursed along my spine. She was near. I couldn't smell her or hear her, but my whiskers quivered in the night's blackness, and the memory of her gentle voice sent soothing ripples through my aching muscles.

You're a good boy ... you don't deserve this.

My heart sped up as I increased my pace, keeping abreast of the car. The car sped up too, as though trying to outrun me. Escape me. My trembling legs worked harder, my paws pounding the soft ground, earthy smells rising around me with each impact.

You're a good boy.

Soon the car headlights eclipsed the moon, became the moon, causing my senses to reel, to unravel, to vaporise like river mist in the sun. Why was I chasing her, the human female? Humans were my deadliest enemy, the one creature on earth I truly feared. But her voice ... her scent. Her warmth. Her defiant spirit.

She called to me, sparking a need that was far stronger and far more ancient than my fear.

7

MAEVE

INSTEAD OF HEADING to Nan's, I detoured past the turnoff and took the road back towards town. Once, I'd loved driving along this scenic route, but not anymore.

The darkness was all-consuming out here.

No street lights, and Riverwood was a few miles south, down the mountainside on the very edge of the forest. I had lived here all my life and for the most part loved it. Or at least I had before I married into the Lamb family. Alec had been so charming at first. Attentive and protective, and I'd lapped it up, loving the way I felt cocooned in his big arms, safe from the world. Nan had told me to marry someone like him. Someone who would look after me.

Protect me.

Shield me.

Give me the security I'd lacked growing up.

"Just don't fall in love with him," she'd warned.

A sob erupted from my throat. An ugly sound, ragged and raw. Then the tears I'd been holding back began to pour out in a torrent.

Alec's not here to protect you now, sweetie.

I sobbed again, a strangled howl as grief engulfed me. But was it grief, though? Really? Or was it something darker, something I'd been suppressing for so long that it had the taste of grief but was something else completely? Guilt, maybe. Or a memory. Clamping the back of my throat so tightly I couldn't breathe.

My brother had his moments, Mae. You of all people should know that.

The car lurched forward as my foot pressed the pedal as if trying to outrun what was coming. I was starting to spiral. Letting my old hopelessness creep back. I'd paid too much for therapy in the past two years to drop the reins now, but my clash tonight with Derek Lamb had jolted something loose.

Shadows sped along the verge as my headlights chased the darkness. One of my windows started to rattle. I should slow down. There were bends ahead.

I gripped the steering wheel tightly, swerving back and forth on the winding road as panic took control. The dense forest seemed to close in as my mind flashed back to the day Alec died.

We're in the forest, camping here for the Easter long weekend, hoping to mend the rift growing between us. It's late at night and he's yelling at me, his breath reeking of drink, his face crimson and his lush lips twisted in anger. "You're a chore to be with, Maeve. Why the hell can't you just stop nagging? Booze isn't my problem. You are." Somehow I'm on the ground, my head spinning, blinking away the sticky wetness that's suddenly pouring down my face—

I startled back to the present as a shadow darted across my headlights. Slamming on the brakes, I screamed as the car fishtailed sideways, tyres screeching on the gravel. The thud of impact jolted me, and I shut my eyes as the car skidded to a stop in the middle of the road.

Shoving open the door, I sprang out and ran back along the verge.

A dog. I'd hit a dog. Killed it probably, if the horrible thump was anything to go by. But where was it? Had it limped off into the bushes to die?

I frowned. A dog. There were no farms near here, so it had to be a feral one—large and grey, shaggy like a wolf, its luminous white eyeshine catching the headlights just before it disappeared.

"Jeez, Mae. Seeing things now?"

I was rattled after clashing with Derek tonight, that was all. Because what were the chances of the same dog—*wolf, Maeve, it was a wolf*—running in front of my car, miles from the sawmill? Yet I could have sworn—

A moan came from behind me.

I spun around, searching the roadside trees. What dog would moan like that? It sounded almost human. Almost. I ran back along the road, and when I saw the pale shape huddled on the verge, I stopped in my tracks.

"What—?"

A man lay there. On his side, his face pushed into the grass, his arms before him. Naked as the day he was born, his skin streaked with blood, his longish hair tangled over his face.

"Hey, are you okay?"

Stupid question. He was clearly not okay. I'd killed him, hadn't I? Killed an innocent man because I lost the plot back there on the road. Dr Palmer had warned me not to drive when I was spiralling. Why didn't I listen? I was no better than Derek. Worse, because he only killed dogs, while I'd just run down some poor guy with my freaking Lancer—

He moaned again.

I kneeled by his side, patting my pockets for my phone, realising it was back in the car.

"Hey, hold on, okay? I'll call an ambulance and get help. "

I went to stand, but his hand shot out and surprisingly strong fingers circled my wrist.

"Wait." He cracked open his eyes, narrowing his gaze on my face. "No ambulance."

I jerked back in shock. Less at his words, more at the eerie way his pupils shone almost white in the glow of my headlights, reminding me of the wolf I'd saved earlier—

I shook my head to clear it. "You're hurt. I hit you with my car and you seem..." As my gaze trailed over his muscular body, I noted the purple bruises covering his ribs and his mangled, bloody wrist. Worst of all was the puncture-like hole near his hip, flowing blood. "Is that a bullet wound?"

Not that I'd ever seen one up close, but Nan's father had once shown me a scar that he said was from the Korean War. It looked like something this could eventually turn into. A deep ragged puncture, the surrounding skin already bruising, and black blood weeping from it in a steady stream.

As I met his gaze, he blinked and the eyeshine faded. His eyes were still pale, but a more natural colour, grey or maybe green, impossible to tell in the gloom.

"No doctor," he said gruffly, propping himself on one elbow as if intending to stand. "Just go away. Leave me alone. I'm fine."

My lips dropped apart. "Go away?"

"My house is nearby. Please, just go. It's not safe for you here."

"Are you kidding me?"

I wanted to laugh, but a part of me wanted to cry as well. Instead, I just stared. I knew him. He was local to Riverwood, but of course my brain was drawing a blank right now. What did he mean, not safe? Were the people who did this coming back for round two?

All the more reason to get him to safety.

I climbed to my feet and searched the road. One way then the other. Beyond the glow of my headlights, the forest road was cloaked in a darkness so dense it seemed tangible, almost alive. Like a large black woolly beast crouching ready to spring.

I looked back at the man. "Can you stand?"

He was already struggling upright, suddenly looming tall beside me, more like a mythical creature with his incredible physique and beautiful, sharp-featured face, blood trickling from a cut near his lip.

He swayed sideways and his arm came out to balance himself, and I grabbed his hand. As I ducked under his arm and pulled it around my shoulders, pressing against his side to steady him, the intense heat of his body shocked me.

"You're burning up." I shivered. "Besides, I'm not going anywhere. What sort of a creep do you think I am? Run a man over and then leave him to bleed out on the roadside? Seriously, I was raised better than that."

He looked at me puzzled, his face close to mine. Was he drunk? I couldn't smell liquor, but he seemed disoriented, almost groggy.

Then his gaze sharpened, not so luminous now, more focussed, as if suddenly seeing me. A soft, husky chuckle rippled through him, sounding almost like a growl. Then he swayed sideways again, and I had to hold him more tightly to stop him from dragging us both over. He lowered his head, resting it against my shoulder, his face nestling into my neck.

Okay. This was weird.

A hot feeling fanned through me. Two years had passed since a man had been this close. It didn't seem to matter that he was a total stranger, that we were miles from town in the darkest stretch of the forest road. Just that his warmth was seeping into my bones and the smoky, clean scent of his skin was making me tremble with something I hadn't felt in a long time.

If ever.

I heard him sigh and then breathe deeply in.

As if he was inhaling me.

And me not scared at all, just standing there on the road, holding him upright. Feeling strangely empowered, and even a little wild, like someone who could, just maybe, let down her hair and dance in the rain. It was a crazy feeling. Unfamiliar. Forbidden. Yet somehow, I didn't want it to end.

I shut my eyes, waiting for all the old warnings to start assaulting me. *Stay on the straight and narrow, Maeve. You know what happens to girls who stray.* But for once the voices were silent. Standing there on the verge with my arms around this large, bleeding, naked man, who had himself tried to warn me away, I felt calm. Unshakeable. I had wandered away from the path, maybe so far away that I'd never again be able to find my way back. But it didn't matter.

Maybe it hadn't mattered all along.

8

———————

FEN

I HAD TRIED to warn her, hadn't I? So why was she helping me into the passenger seat of her car? A woman alone in the desolate night with a stranger. A dangerous stranger who could turn at any moment and tear her to shreds? Jeez, did the woman have no fear?

Unexpected admiration flooded me.

I hated myself for feeling it because I should be trying to send her away, not congratulate her. The night wasn't over. The moon was yet to set. Until the last inky threads of darkness drained away and the moon sank behind the distant hills, she was not safe.

From me.

She disappeared for a moment, opening the car boot and returning with a tartan picnic rug. Unfolding it, she placed it over me, tucking it gently around me, covering my nakedness.

"Just so you know," she said sternly. "I'm not at all okay with you going straight home." She had a pleasant, slightly husky voice that sent tingles down my spine. "You need urgent medical attention. It looks like you've lost a lot of blood."

"I'll be fine." And I would be, once I was alone and didn't have to worry about mauling her. "I could walk home from here."

She sighed, shaking her head. "The least I can do is drive you. You said you live nearby? There's just the old Harkness place on Whitefeather Road, but that's been empty for years."

"It's not empty."

"Oh." Her eyes widened, her brows swooping as she fixed on my face with new interest. "You live there? Are you a friend of the family? I heard there was a nephew somewhere, is that you?"

I sighed. So many questions. My life was already over-complicated. I didn't need anyone excavating the past. Speculating about my personal life and putting us both in danger. The sort of danger that ruined not just lives but generations.

I inhaled to give her my usual spiel, but her nearness caught me off guard. Her breath was sweet like chocolate, and a faint floral scent radiated off her skin, lavender maybe, mingling with the salty perspiration the night's heat had drawn from her pores.

I dragged my top teeth over my lip. "I'm Fen Harkness."

She seemed taken off guard, too. "From the vet clinic?"

"Yeah."

She frowned, leaning closer as if myopic, searching my features. "Then we've already met. I thought you seemed familiar. I brought you a lorikeet last year. You've probably forgotten."

I knew exactly who she was.

Married into the Lamb family straight from high school, keeping to herself. Hiding the bruises inflicted by a husband who always seemed to reek of booze. Loyal to the clan I had spent my life hating.

I narrowed my eyes. "Lorikeet?"

"I found it outside the school with a broken wing. You reset its bones, and kept it at the shelter till it healed. I'm Maeve, by the way." She held out her hand, probably intending that we shake like any normal introduction, only this was anything but normal.

Here I was buck naked in her car, bleeding onto her sheepskin seat cover and now probably staining up her picnic rug as well. Still feeling the call of the wild in my veins as I battled to ignore the sweet dark light of the moon.

I patted my throbbing hip, nodding at the road.

"I'm feeling a bit lightheaded. Any chance of that lift?"

She pulled back, grimacing. "Oh, heck! You're right, the car's reeking of blood and you're probably in a lot of pain right now. And here am I rabbiting on about lorikeets."

She tugged the rug up higher around me, its rough wool scraping my skin, and despite the summer heat I shivered. My senses were still acute. It was dark inside the car but I could see the black pools her enlarged irises made of her eyes, and hear the quick pitapat of her heart. Sense the gentle throb of the large juicy vein in her neck.

The animal in me stirred.

Getting hit by the car had made it retreat, but now, with her so close, with temptation howling through my body like a cyclone, I trod a fine line. Dawn was still hours away, and in that time anything could happen.

Shoving off the rug, I reached for the door handle.

"On second thoughts, I'm just gonna—"

Her small fingers settled on my forearm. "Please don't go. I'd feel really bad about leaving you here. To be honest, I've had a shitty night. Let me balance out the bad by doing something good, okay?"

This was a terrible idea.

But how could I refuse her pleading eyes?

I gazed through the windscreen at the night, trying to block out the sound of my thundering heart ... and suddenly my ribs and hip and ankle, my throbbing forearm, every bruise and scrape and cut, every humiliation I'd endured tonight, seemed to defeat me.

I sagged back in the seat.

"How are you with a needle and thread?"

She smiled, relief relaxing her features. "Surprisingly good." She settled behind the wheel, buckling up and starting the ignition. "I made this blouse myself, believe it or not. My nan taught me, she was a wonderful seamstress in her day..."

She cut off, blinking, then glanced over at me, her smile gone. Her gaze travelled down the picnic rug and settled on the patch of blood that was already seeping into the thick wool from the wound on my hip.

"Oh," she said so meekly I almost felt sorry for her. "You weren't talking about that sort of stitching, were you?"

I didn't reply, so weary all of a sudden that I could only sag deeper against the backrest and shut my eyes. As we drove, the forest whispered through the open window and the moon sang to me, its song full of warning. *You can't let your guard down, it's too dangerous. Remember what happened before? How will you live with yourself if it happens again?*

9

MAEVE

FEN'S HOUSE was impressively large, a tantalising Gothic double-story straight from the pages of a dark fairytale. The roof pitched high like a forbidden mountain, with towering windows that were tight-lipped and uninviting. It was cloaked in darkness, no lights daring to break the mystery.

I braced myself for an equally brooding interior, but once inside, the vibe shifted. Fen switched on a lamp and soft yellow light flooded the large room, illuminating the sleek modern furniture and stunning wildlife photography adorning every wall. His collection of antique birdcages added a touch of whimsy, their shadows striping the white walls like delicate prison bars.

Being at home seemed to revive Fen. While I was busy looking around, he limped into another room and came back wearing grey track pants and a towel wadded against his bleeding hip, carrying a first aid kit and a bowl of antiseptic. He sank onto the couch with a grunt, placing the kit on the floor.

I sat beside him on the leather couch, the cushions creaking under me. He peeled off the towel so we could examine the gunshot wound on his hip.

He'd been right about his injury. The bullet had sliced clean through. I slithered onto the floor by his side, dipping some gauze in the antiseptic and tracing it lightly over his torn flesh. Alec had been a sook, wincing and moaning the one time he'd gotten in a bar fight, so I had learned to be gentle.

Fen glared at me. "You need to use more pressure," he growled.

His irritation rolled over me in waves, making me swipe at the wound more vigorously as I mopped the fresh ooze of blood—although he seemed unbothered. As I picked up the tiny suture needle and hooked it through one ragged edge of the skin, my fingers started to shake. The first stitch took forever. Finally, I knotted it and snipped the thread, easing out a sigh of relief.

"That's one."

"One?" Fen grumbled. "I could've done it quicker myself."

My teeth gnashed together. "You'd have had trouble reaching back this far."

"I've tackled worse."

The needle hovered precariously over his wound, quivering in my unsteady fingers. Arrogant prick. I glared up at him, wanting to snap back but biting my tongue. Making eye contact felt somehow dangerous, like watching a storm brew. A nasty, violent thunderstorm that any sensible person would stay out of.

I swallowed. "I get how you could take a bullet in the middle of a forest, and even get so torn up. But how on earth did you lose all your clothes?"

His eyes gleamed darkly. "None of your damn business."

I bit my lips in annoyance. Okay. Now my mind was spinning out of control. A love tryst gone wrong. A gang revenge, though I knew of no gangs in Riverwood. Or maybe—

He cleared his throat. "I can hear the cogs turning."

"I'm curious, that's all."

"And we all know what happens to little cats who get too curious."

I hooked the next few sutures more vigorously and tied them off, snipping the black thread with a flourish.

"You'd still be limping home if it wasn't for me. You might have bled out or fainted again."

"I didn't faint. You struck me with your car and I was—"

"Stunned? Like a sparrow hitting the window?"

A low sound rumbled from his chest as he glared at me. For a moment, the fierce luminosity came back into his eyes but quickly faded. They were green, I noted. His eyes. Pale, silvery green like frozen river water.

He let out a pained sigh. "Aren't you finished yet?"

I bent closer to examine the ragged wound on his forearm. "Your wrist. Lord, you're lucky it's not broken. Looks like something bit you."

I took out a clean suture needle and swabs, then settled beside him on the couch. He rested his hand palm up on my lap while I stitched the torn skin. Black bruises covered the surrounding skin, and I was dying to ask, but I bit my lips, knowing he'd only brush me off again. I bandaged it in silence and sat back.

"Looks like it should do the trick."

"It will."

"Listen, if you insist on not seeing a doctor, then at least get some comfrey balm to put on your wounds. I wouldn't normally recommend it for anything deep, but it'll speed up recovery."

"Thanks," he said gruffly, rising to his feet and collecting the first aid kit. Looking anywhere but at me.

A headache was starting to nag behind my eyes. I remembered some leftover chocolate cake in my fridge at home and suddenly wished I was eating it instead of being stuck here.

"Well, I guess I'll head off. I hope you feel better soon." Actually, I hoped the ungrateful bastard would rot in hell, but of course I kept that part to myself.

He moved towards a door at the back of the room, his bare feet padding softly on the hardwood floor.

"Hey."

I risked a glance up. "What?"

"I want to show you something."

Uh-oh. Show me what, exactly? Hadn't I already seen enough? In my mind, I stepped back, seeing the big picture. A naked man, beaten and shot, found in the woods. And the ninny who not only gave him a lift home but pulled a Florence Nightingale by agreeing to patch him up. I had strayed off the path—big time—and no one knew I was here.

"Uh, you know ... I'm just gonna go."

"Do you like owls?"

My head jerked back, my lips parting. "I freaking love owls! How did you know?"

"That lorikeet you brought in last year? I figured you must be a bird fancier. Come on, it's a female southern boobook. She's a real beauty."

I followed him out to a huge undercover deck at the back of the house. A long wooden Bali lounge stacked with cushions sat along the wall beneath an array of antique tools—old scythes and secateurs—and beyond that was a long redwood dining set. At the far end, several large wire cages were assembled under the wide roof. Only one was occupied. A small white owl with brown markings lifted her wings when she saw us, hooting softly.

"She's gorgeous," I whispered going up to the cage. "Her wing—what's wrong with it?"

"It was broken, though she's mending well. A friend of mine rescued her from a dog trap a few weeks ago."

I cringed. A dog trap, possibly laid by Derek Lamb. To catch the wolves he hated.

That we both hated.

I swallowed. "She was lucky someone found her in time. She might have starved. Or been ... mauled."

Fen's eyes caught mine in the gloom, his features softening.

"My friend rescues a lot of wildlife," he murmured. "He brings them in, I patch them up. And then we send them back out."

"I hate that the traps catch animals other than wolves."

His arms shifted as if suppressing a shiver.

"We rescue wolves too." It sounded like a challenge. "They might not be native wildlife, but they have their place in nature. They feel pain and fear like everyone else."

A strange choice of words, *everyone* else, as if he was talking about people. It made me think of the wolf I freed tonight. The way his eyes gleamed, the way he'd gentled at the sound of my voice.

"I hate that it has to be so cruel. But those wild dogs do a lot of damage. Not just to possums and birds, but to..." My words drifted off, my throat suddenly tight, and I had to swallow before going on. "But sometimes to people."

"I heard about your husband."

I waited for him to say how sorry he was, maybe that he'd known Alec and what a shame to have his life cut short in such a senseless way.

Instead, the silence stretched. I glanced over. He was

watching me, not casually like someone I barely knew, but staring with an intensity that should have been scary. But somehow wasn't.

"Hey," he said, almost in a whisper. "Would you like to help me release her—"

A deafening crash shook the entire house, shattering the stillness. The owl let out a panicked screech and fluttered her wings.

Fen bolted down the verandah steps and towards the front of the house and I quickly followed, afraid that my car parked on the dark verge had been sideswiped. All we saw was a set of tail lights disappearing into the darkness.

"Damn it," I said, rushing over to check my Lancer, relieved to find it unscathed. "You've really pissed someone off tonight, haven't you?"

Fen bounded up onto the front verandah, looking around. Shards of glass littered the deck, along with a large chunk of brick sitting under the smashed front window. He sighed, dragging fingers through his thick hair as he gazed around at the mess.

"I can't imagine who'd do this."

I shrugged, wrapping my arms around myself.

"Maybe the same people who shot you tonight? Just saying."

10

MAEVE

PULLING the brush through my tangled hair, I stared into the mirror, still groggy after another restless night. Two large possum eyes blinked sleepily back at me, the tiny freckles dancing over my nose and cheeks making me seem way younger than my thirty-two years.

I was running late. Again.

Kitty would have to open the shop, and my excuse of over-sleeping was wearing thin, even to me. But that was the least of my worries—it was the dark shadows under my eyes that told the real story.

For almost a week, Fen Harkness had been haunting my dreams. From the moment I shut my eyes till the blare of my alarm clock, all I seemed to see was his muscular body bathed in moonlight as he sprawled on the roadside, his skin streaked with blood. The way he'd leaned against me, inhaling me as if aware, like me, of the electric connection between us. And then on the back verandah with the owl, his whisper in the darkness. *Hey, would you like to help me release her...*

Blowing out a breath, I snapped an elastic around my ponytail.

I should be focusing on other things—like restocking my shop with fresh native seeds to replace the old stale ones. Or dealing with Derek and the wild dog dilemma, or figuring out how to brave the forest again.

But no.

Here I was obsessing over a man I'd known for five minutes, my sleep-deprived brain whirling with questions. Who had bashed him on Friday night, leaving him for dead on the roadside? Were they locals, and if so, what grudge could they hold against a harmless veterinarian? He seemed like an okay guy despite his grumpiness. Rescuing owls and saving wildlife. Weird that he insisted on me stitching him up instead of seeing a medic, though. And why would someone smash his window?

Nan might know.

She knew everyone in Riverwood—and all their secrets. The trick would be getting her to spill the beans. I brushed on some mascara and covered my lips in pomegranate balm, then rang Kitty.

"I'll be in after lunch. Can you manage to keep the place afloat without me till then?"

"Quitter," she accused. "Give Nan a hug from me, and tell her she did a terrible job raising you."

I laughed. "She raised you worse."

"Drive safe, loser."

I was still chuckling in the kitchen as I tossed some fresh garden produce into a basket. I added some leftover cupcakes from Kitty's last batch and a bottle of homemade myrtle lemonade. Grabbing my car keys, I set off for Nan's.

The forest road was different in full sunlight—the trees gently shaded, their leaves fluttering in a friendly breeze. I craned my neck as I passed the sawmill, but there was no sign of anyone, just a glimpse of the burned-out fire pit.

Nan's house stood high on a hill with stunning river views, and as I climbed the path to her front verandah, I paused to gaze over the forest. From here I could just see the dark crown of my favourite tree in the world, the old-growth spotted gum I had often hiked to before Alec's attack.

A shiver flew up my arms.

I loved that tree. I missed going to see it. Missed the peace and calm that oozed from its ancient trunk and massive branches. It seemed so remote now, so unsafe. Had I really hiked there alone? Unaware of the dangers prowling around me—

"Maeve!"

I flew around, clutching my heart.

Nan stood in her doorway, a frown etching her beautiful features. "Oh, love. Still jumpy, are you?" She had on her gardening smock over a floral dress, her feet bare. A small sprig of flowers nestled in her grey updo, a telltale sign she'd just been tending her plants.

"I'm fine, Nan." I followed her inside, lugging my basket into the kitchen. "It's you I'm worried about. Kitty mentioned you weren't feeling well?"

"I had one of my turns, but I'm feeling better now." She spied the basket and beamed, pulling out the lemonade. "How did you know I was craving this? And are those cupcakes? I think you're trying to spoil your old nan."

I laughed, the tension draining out of my shoulders as I helped her unpack.

"It's a bribe. I need some info."

She turned from the fridge, smiling. "Who are we discussing today?"

Nan preferred living on the outskirts of town, but

somehow she stayed abreast of everything that went on in the community. She wasn't into gossip and never spoke ill of anyone, yet she had a knack for knowing things. Not just about current events, but things from the past as well.

I packed a knobbly sweet potato into a large earthenware bowl in her pantry.

"Fen Harkness, the vet? I found him last night on the forest road, barely conscious. He'd been beaten up. And..." I lowered my voice, feeling weird. "I'm pretty sure he'd been shot at."

Nan turned pale. "Harkness?"

"So you know him?"

Slowly, Nan closed the fridge door. She beckoned me outside to the back patio, where sunlight streamed through thick vines growing through the roof beams. We sank into deep, comfy chairs.

"I know his family," Nan said at last. She must have sensed the blossom caught in her hair because she patted the strands until she found it. "Or at least, know of them. Young Fen's the only one left these days. Sad about his parents."

"What happened to them?"

Nan twirled the sprig in her fingers, watching me, her blue eyes thoughtful.

"His parents died quite young. A hunting accident. So they said."

"What do you mean?"

"Emeric was a farmer. Such a sweet, peaceful man. Hunting repulsed him, so that can't have been the reason they were in the forest that night. Whatever he and Evelina were doing in the deep woods is anyone's guess. But the pair of them, gone. Just like that. Fen was fourteen, his sister sixteen. Poor Erin never recovered from their deaths. Fen worked afternoons and weekends out at the stables on Rawsons Road, and Erin did whatever she could to keep them together in the family home. Child services were onto them, pressing for them to enter foster care. We offered to take them in, but Erin was almost rabid in her desperation for them to stay out at White-feather Road."

"Why?"

"No idea, love. It made no sense."

"Huge responsibility for a teenager."

Nan nodded. "It gets worse, though. By the time Erin was seventeen, she started losing her grip. Skipping school, drinking alcohol. Getting into trouble with the police. You remember when I volunteered at the medical centre? Well, she started coming in, rambling about a family curse. Saying her parents didn't die by accident, that they'd been killed because of it."

"Sounds like grief."

"It was more than that, Maeve." Nan looked down at the sprig she was still twirling. "There are forces in this town that no one speaks about, dark forces."

I sat up, looking at her. "What are you talking about?"

She shrugged, finally looking across at me. "I think you should stay away from Fen Harkness."

A feeling like panic gripped me as I flickered back to Friday night on the forest road. Fen's face inches from mine, the way he nuzzled close like he'd done it a thousand times before. It felt like he was either looking for comfort or trying to give me some. We weren't supposed to be anything but strangers, yet some-how, it felt like we were anything but. It made no sense, yet somehow it totally did.

"It sounds like he needs a friend, Nan."

"Perhaps he does, Maeve. But trust me, that friend won't be you."

"Why?"

"For one thing, the Harkness family always hated the Lambs. I've no idea how Emeric made an enemy of old Betty

Lamb, but he ruffled her feathers somehow and she never forgave him."

"But that's another generation."

"Blood runs thick in this town, love. You probably know that better than anyone."

I slumped back. Maybe that explained Fen's coolness towards me the other night. If one of the Lambs was guilty of attacking him, of course he'd be wary of me. I was a Lamb by marriage, despite having kept my own name, and everyone in town knew it.

"Do you think the family feud is ongoing?"

"It's possible." Nan twirled the blossom. "Quite likely, knowing how tightly the Lambs hold their grudges."

"Betty Lamb always struck me as a bit of a witch." I smiled, trying to lighten things up, even as a prickle of unease went over me. "Maybe *she* cursed Fen's family?"

Nan crumpled the sprig of tiny blooms in her fingers and let the fragments sift onto the deck.

"Erin Harkness believed in that curse with all her heart. Who are we to say it wasn't real? How do we know that it didn't pass down from one family member to another? That if you get involved with Fen, it won't somehow pass onto you?"

My mouth dropped open. "But, Nan—"

"But nothing, Maeve. Stay away from him, you hear?"

"Because of a stupid curse? But he's nice."

"So was Alec at the start."

Ouch. That was below the belt. I'd never told her about Alec's drinking. Never told her about all the blowups we had, always wanting to protect her. Had she known all along?

I let out a heavy sigh. "Alec was a decent guy, Nan. Everyone's got their issues."

"Not like the Harknesses," she shot back, her eyes steely. "Promise you won't get mixed up with him?"

I gave a reluctant nod. "All right."

But as I hugged her goodbye and dashed down the steps to my car, I couldn't shake the image of a teenage Fen. Sweating under the blazing Riverwood sun, mucking out stable yards with the burden of the world on his young shoulders, he and his sister struggling to hold their family together.

As I cruised along the sun-dappled forest road, my brain buzzed. How did a soft-spoken vet from a sleepy country town become the sort of person with enemies ruthless enough to leave him for dead in the woods?

11

MAEVE

As I navigated the winding road along the bush reserve near my house, I noticed a flicker of movement beneath the canopy of roadside trees. I eased off the gas, peering through the windscreen. A shadowy, four-legged shape wove stealthily between the trunks, momentarily caught by the dappled afternoon sunlight filtering through the leaves.

"What the...?"

I tapped the brakes, veering closer to the verge. Suddenly, a big grey dog—wait, no, it was a wolf—emerged from the shadows and locked eyes with me, almost like it knew me, its white muzzle flashing in the sun.

I eased back onto the road, frowning. It looked like the same one I saved from the mill the other night.

"That's just crazy."

But as I pulled into my driveway, the wolf lingered in the nearby trees, edging closer. A shiver ran through me. What was it after? Had it picked up my scent from the forest and followed me home like a stray? The wolf's ears pricked up suddenly and it slipped among the shadows, disappearing back into the reserve.

As I got out and dashed up my driveway, the sound of another car approached. I turned back, my heart sinking when I saw the familiar white ute pull up to the curb. Derek Lamb climbed out and headed straight for me, raising his meaty arm in a wave. I sent a nervous look around for the wolf, but it had vanished.

Derek narrowed his eyes, trailing his gaze over me.

"Why'd you hit up the vet's place the other night after I saw you? Needed someone to whine to?"

My neck tensed. "Were you spying on me?"

"Just looking out for you. Everyone knows Harkness is against putting down the dogs. I figured you'd be the last person to cosy up to him."

"I wasn't cosying up. I gave him a ride home, that's all. Why were you following me?"

"I suppose you'll hook up with him now? Poor Alec's hardly cold in his grave, and you're already on the prowl."

I wanted to laugh, or scream, or maybe ball up my fist and take a swing at Derek's annoying face. Instead, I inhaled a calming breath.

"Not that it's any of your business," I said through gritted teeth. "But no. We're not hooking up. Fen Harkness is the last guy I'd want anything to do with." *Except you*, I almost added, but bit my tongue. Then it clicked. "You were the one who smashed his window."

Derek shrugged like it was nothing. "He had it coming, Mae. Always going on about saving the bloody wolves while my little brother's been gone for two years. Harkness is useless. It should've been him buried, not Alec."

The sudden rawness in his face, the gleam of tears, disarmed me. For all his bluster, Derek had adored his brother.

I slumped as my anger deflated.

"He's a vet, Derek. He patches up all kinds of animals, not just wolves. From what I hear, he pays regular visits to Reg Garrett's farm to help with lambing his stubborn ewes."

Derek shook his head, scraping a thumb under his eye. "I don't care, Mae. How can you not hate those mongrel wolves as much as I do? After what happened to my brother, it doesn't seem right."

My gaze strayed to the line of trees by my fence, and the shadows swarming there.

"For two years, I've been terrified of them. You know that. Just thinking about returning to the forest made me physically ill. But I got over it, Derek. I moved on. I don't want to live my life in the past. It's not healthy."

Derek traced where I was looking, his brow furrowing deeper. When he turned back to me, his eyes simmered with fury.

"What's not healthy is a Lamb getting friendly with a Harkness."

"I'm not a Lamb, Derek. I kept Nan's surname, remember."

"Alec was one of us, and marrying him makes you one too."

"I'll never be one of you," I said, more hotly than I meant to. "I'm a Winters, and no matter what you or anyone else says, that's not gonna change."

Derek's face turned hard. "Then you're a nobody, Maeve. A foster kid no one wanted. And a bloody fool. Honestly, I sometimes wonder why Alec married you when he could have had any girl in town. And this is how you repay him." He puffed up and leaned in close, casting his shadow over me. "That wolf you let loose on Friday? It's mine tonight. I'm waging war now, Maeve. By the end of the month, there won't be a single one of your precious wild dogs left in Riverwood—or anywhere nearby." He turned to go, then looked back. "Maybe if you're a good little girl, I'll save you a pelt."

He stormed back to his car, the engine roaring to life as he sped off down the street. I glared after him, my legs shaking under me, my vision blurring as tears stung my eyes.

"I hated Alec," I whispered childishly, swiping the dampness from my cheek. "I hate all you Lambs. I hope the wolves come and eat every last one of you, even your cranky old grandma."

A twig snapped nearby and I whipped around, my jaw dropping when I spotted the grey wolf just a few body lengths away.

He had emerged from the shadows and stood by the fence in my yard, ears pricked, bathed in daylight, bold and beautiful as the sun.

I snapped my mouth shut, wishing I could take back my words and the terrible secret that had made me say them. But before I could react, the wolf dashed off and disappeared into the reserve as swiftly as he'd appeared.

12

FEN

THURSDAY WAS one of our busiest days at the animal hospital unless there was an emergency callout, and so far, I'd mended a parrot's wing, desexed a cocker spaniel and treated two cats for ear infections. And it wasn't even lunchtime.

When the door opened, I barely glanced up.

Then did a double-take.

It was her. Maeve. The one I hadn't stopped thinking about for the past week. I blinked, not sure if she was real or if my mind was playing tricks on me. She raised a hand in greeting as she made her way towards me through the bustling waiting room.

"Maeve." Hell, what was wrong with me? Did I have to sound so gruff?

"Fen." Her lips tightened as she gave me the once-over. "How are you feeling?"

She was even more breathtaking in daylight if that was possible. Even with the stark fluorescent lights washing out her features, she looked even more luscious than she had last week on the forest road. The mascara streaks were gone, her dark auburn hair brushed back from her face, her amber eyes bright as autumn leaves. The green vintage dress skimming her curves was begging my gaze to linger.

I backtracked, trying to remember her question.

"Yeah, I'm good."

Her frown gravitated to my hip. "Your stitches?"

"Almost ready to come out."

"Are you sure? It's only been a week—"

When she spied the ragged pink scar above my wrist, she grabbed my arm, her small, strong fingers trapping me.

"Wait. How did this heal so quickly?"

"I guess it wasn't as bad as we thought."

"It was really deep. I should know, I stitched it closed."

I leaned in as if to tell a secret. "I tried the comfrey balm. You're right. It works miracles. Anyway, why are you here?"

She slumped, her brow wrinkling. "Do you have a minute?"

"Yeah, sure."

She glanced over her shoulder. "Maybe somewhere less public?"

I nodded and led her through the back door to the kennels, my pulse quickening as we stepped into the narrow yard. What was she doing here? Had she come to see me? The thought sent a thrill through my body, followed by a pang of guilt. I shouldn't be feeling this way, not after what happened the other night. Being around me was putting her in the sort of danger I couldn't bear thinking about.

As we entered the yard, one of the rescue dogs started barking, setting off the others. We currently had five dogs, plus a koala and a family of blue tongue lizards, all needing round-the-clock care. The barking faded as Liam walked between the cages, quieting the dogs with a glance or gentle word.

"Who's he?" Maeve wanted to know.

"Liam Belrose, my nurse."

Her eyes widened. "It wasn't him who beat you up the other night, was it?"

I bit my lip, shooting a glance towards my offsider. "He gets that a lot. But no, under the Rammstein T-shirt and tats, he's a cool guy. My best mate."

Her shoulders sagged. "I didn't mean to judge."

"His baby bro is a cop, so he gets that a lot." I led her back along the side of the building to a patch of sunlight. "How can I help?"

She took a deep breath. "A wolf is hanging around my place, and I was hoping you—"

The scrape of boots on concrete made me turn. Liam had followed us, a rescue pup cradled against his chest like it weighed nothing. The contrast between his scarred knuckles and the gentle way he stroked the dog's ears wasn't lost on me— or Maeve, judging by how she stared.

"So you're the one causing trouble," Liam said, roving his gaze over her. The pup squirmed and he adjusted his hold, revealing the wolf's head inked on his forearm. "Fen won't shut up about you."

I shot him a warning look. "Don't you have meds to prep?"

"Already done." He stepped closer, and I caught the familiar scent of pine needles and worn leather. "Overheard you've got a wolf problem. Might be able to help with that."

Maeve's eyes darted between us. "You know about wolves?"

"You could say that." The corner of his mouth lifted. "Family business."

I cleared my throat. "Liam traps for the wildlife service sometimes." It wasn't exactly a lie. "But this is my case."

He shrugged, but I knew that look in his eyes. He was measuring her up, making judgements of his own, no doubt less innocent than the ones Maeve had made about him. The pup in his arms yawned, showing tiny teeth, and Maeve's expression softened.

"Can I?" she asked, reaching for the dog.

Liam passed it over with surprising grace for someone his size. "Careful. She's still healing." His fingers brushed Maeve's as he transferred the pup, and I felt a growl building in my throat that I quickly swallowed.

"Liam found her in the national park last week. Someone left her for dead."

"That's awful," Maeve whispered, cradling the pup. "Who would do that?"

"Same kind who'd shoot a wolf on sight." Liam's voice had gone hard. He caught my eye, and I saw the flash of silver there. "Good thing she's got people looking out for her now."

Maeve gave the pup back, and we watched Liam stride back to the cages, the little dog snug in his arms.

Maeve turned to me. "So, that grey wolf at my place. Can you catch it?"

I swayed back, my senses sharpening as I inhaled the sweet, floral scent from her skin, tinged with a faint sharpness. Fear. Of course she was scared—after witnessing her husband's attack two years ago.

"It won't hurt you, Maeve. It's probably hunting rabbits. Just don't approach it, okay?"

She huffed. "I'm not scared of him. Well, maybe a little. But I'm more scared *for* him."

"Why?"

"My brother-in-law is on the warpath. Did you know he's been culling the wild dogs?"

I nodded at our rows of cages. "We've saved plenty of dogs from traps. Left there to bleed out or die of starvation. Or worse. Not many wolves, though."

"Oh?"

"Wolves are cautious and have a strong sense of smell. The only way they'd get trapped is if something—or someone—distracted them."

Maeve shuddered. "It's not that I'm against the culling, as long as it's done humanely. It's just—"

"Just?"

"There's something about the grey wolf. He's special somehow."

Huh, special. "Maybe he wants to be friends," I said, smiling and puffing up a bit—then I cringed. *You idiot, that's the last idea you should be putting in her head.*

"Friends? With a wolf?" Maeve raised a brow, her honey-brown eyes searching mine. "Is that even possible? Wolves aren't exactly domesticated pets."

I shrugged, choosing my next words more carefully. "They're complex creatures. Intelligent, social, with strong family bonds. Maybe it senses you're not a threat."

She huffed. "That's the problem. I'm more of a threat than it knows. It's my fault Derek's targeting it, and we have to do something."

I had a sinking feeling I already knew the answer but had to ask anyway.

"Why's it your fault?"

"He trapped it the other night. He and his mates were tormenting it, so I set it free. Now Derek thinks I've betrayed him."

"Because of how your husband died?"

She nodded. "Look, Derek's my brother-in-law. I know him pretty well. Unfortunately," she added to herself and sighed. "He won't give up till he's tortured and killed the poor thing. We have to help it."

A warm feeling bloomed in my chest, and I bit down a smile. *She cares about that mangy dog, dammit. Really cares.*

But it was more than just pride.

As I swayed towards her, the shadows inside me stirred as if a primal thing was awakening. Liam often talked about imprinting—about meeting your twin soul. None of us ever had, though he'd made it sound intense and wonderful, yet also like a jail sentence. *Bro, you just sense it, okay? Like finding the missing part of yourself, and once you do, it lasts for life.*

Was that the magnetic pull I felt the other night as Maeve crouched beside me, stitching me up? The unexpected feelings that prickled my defenses and made me so grouchy? What I'd felt in the car, or even earlier by the side of the road, inhaling her in the dark?

She trailed her gaze along the kennels. "Are they all rescues?"

I cleared my throat. "Pretty much."

"Any wild dogs?"

"Some."

"Wolves?"

A pause. "Occasionally."

"What happens when they recover?"

"We relocate them. Liam's mum owns a bush property west of here. Forty thousand hectares. Liam rescues the critters—birds, snakes, possums, and yeah, even the wild dogs—and I patch them up. When they're ready for release, we take them out to Clearhaven and set them free."

She frowned. "Aren't you worried the dogs will eat all the wildlife?"

"They eat some, but that's nature for you."

"They're wiping out our native animals, you know."

"Lack of habitat is wiping them out, Maeve. Cutting down forests for grazing. Building houses and driving out prey animals, and then culling the natural predators when they attack livestock." I sighed. "Okay, rant over."

"So you'll help me catch the wolf and relocate it?"

Her eyes shone with hope, her pink lips curving sweetly, her little teeth so white and her freckles dancing in the sunlight, that my blood began to roar in my veins. We could spend the whole day searching and still never spot the grey wolf. He didn't want to be found, so we wouldn't find him. But I couldn't say any of that, so I just nodded.

"Sure."

Maeve squinted, shading her eyes with her hand and looking at me with such admiration that right then I'd have happily laid down and died for her.

13

MAEVE

"He's been hanging around here." I pointed to the soft earth near my side fence, that ran along beside the nature reserve. "See? Fresh tracks."

Fen crouched to examine the prints, the late afternoon sunlight casting him in shadows.

"Wolves usually steer clear of people. He'll probably move on in a day or so. No need to trap him."

"But what if he doesn't? What if Derek sees him?"

"Then call Liam. He's an experienced trapper." Fen straightened, his shoulder brushing mine, his eyes serious. "Just be careful, okay? If he approaches, back away slowly. Don't make eye contact, he'll see it as a threat. Above all else, stay calm."

I chewed my lip. "He seems kind of friendly."

"Trust me, he's not." Fen's voice hardened. "He's an apex predator who can chew through a human thigh bone in two or three bites."

"Oh." My legs wobbled as that image burst into my mind, somehow morphing into Alec's face that night in the forest, twisting in shock as the powerful shadow-beast flew at him, dragging him down—

Warm fingers gripped my arm. "Maeve?"

I tried to swallow, but my tongue seemed glued to the roof of my mouth. Fen's hand lingered, his thumb smoothing my skin, his warmth seeping through me.

"I'm sorry," he said quietly. "I don't need to tell you how brutal they can be."

I hugged myself, exhaling a shudder. "You're right. I was getting ahead of myself. It's just that I feel calm when I see him. As if something inside me knows he won't hurt me."

A shadow passed across Fen's face. "He won't hurt you, Maeve."

"But you said—"

He seemed to catch himself, the shutters coming down behind his eyes. "As long as you keep your distance."

Dry leaves crunched under our shoes as we hiked further up the hill behind my house. Something told me the wolf wasn't here, but I had to try. We searched among the tree shadows and headed down into the gully, where a small seasonal creek flowed with clear water from the mountains. Fen stopped to scoop some into his hand and drink.

"What are you doing?" I laughed, skipping around him in horror. "That's creek water. There could be anything in it!"

"It's crystal clear." His eyes gleamed greyish green in the sunlight. "Here, try some." He cupped his hand and collected more water, holding it out like he expected me to lap from his palm.

When I wrinkled my nose, he flicked the water at me, and I ran away shrieking. He chased after me, bounding over the rough terrain with far more ease than me. He seemed to come alive in the wild, as though he belonged here, and I suddenly envied him.

I stopped running and let him catch me. He scooped me lightly around the waist and then released me, his angular face alight with something that took my breath away.

Were we just messing around ... or was it flirting?

I barely knew Fen, but somehow I felt more myself with him than I ever did with Alec. Than with most people, aside from Kitty and Nan. Was this what moving on felt like?

Fen let out a growly chuckle. "It's getting late."

I gazed up at the sky, dismayed to see the sun skimming the distant hills. "It seems like we just got here."

"Night always comes too quickly," he said, almost to himself.

"Scared of the dark, are we?" I teased.

He flashed a grin and reached for my face, stopping me in my tracks as butterflies swarmed through me. At first, I thought it was fear, but when he plucked a leaf from my hair and sent it sailing away into the afternoon on a puff of his breath, the butterflies danced even more wildly, and I realised it was something else entirely.

Something I wasn't even remotely ready to feel.

I turned away and started walking again.

His tread was almost silent beside me.

My boots were small compared to his large ones, but I seemed to be crashing along like a wild elephant while he made hardly any sound at all.

Weird. But I liked his weirdness.

A lot.

We followed the fence line, looking for more signs of the grey wolf. The afternoon sun filtered through the trees, making the dappled shadows dance across Fen's face. He pointed out different animal tracks—possums, wallabies, a goanna that had passed through recently.

"You really know your wildlife." I grinned as he launched

into an explanation of how to tell the age of tracks by their edges.

"Occupational hazard." His eyes crinkled at the corners as he smiled. "Though sometimes I think I prefer animals to people."

"Says the town vet to the plant lady." I bumped his shoulder with mine. "We're quite the pair of hermits."

He laughed, a rich sound that made something warm unfurl in my chest. "At least my patients bite. Yours just sit there looking pretty."

"Clearly you've never dealt with an angry grevillea." I showed him the scratches on my forearms. "They're vicious."

His fingers traced one of the marks, feather-light, and my breath caught. For a moment, the air between us felt charged, electric. I held my breath, mesmerised by his touch, spellbound. The other night he'd been abrupt to the point of rudeness. Now here he was trailing gentle fingers along my skin, arousing goosebumps, sending threads of heat through my limbs.

The sun dipped toward the horizon, the moon appearing like a silver blade on the opposite edge of the darkening sky. Fen's hand dropped away, his expression shuttering.

"We should head back." He stepped away, the familiar distance creeping into his voice. "It'll be dark soon."

"I guess our quarry is long gone."

The silence stretched, so I peeked at him through my lashes. He was scowling at the sky, fixated on the moon. When he noticed me looking, he gave a sad, lopsided smile.

"You're a good person, Maeve. For trying to help the grey wolf. Most people can't stand them, and I get why. You've got more reason than most to hate them. Yet you don't."

I nodded, but my throat was suddenly too tight to say anything. So, I just managed a small, awkward smile, and for the rest of the walk back to the house we were like strangers again, silent and lost in ourselves, as if our easy banter before had never happened.

I dawdled for a moment, watching him stride ahead, all business now, the playful man from moments ago gone. Was he always hot and cold like this? Why did he keep pulling away just when I started to feel close to him?

I made myself a promise.

I'm going to find out.

14

———

MAEVE

I WAS up to my elbows in potting mix the following morning, when the bell above the door chimed. I glanced up, expecting Kitty or perhaps a regular customer. Instead, Betty Lamb stood at the threshold, elegant in a cream-colored pantsuit and high heels.

"Betty." I wiped my hands on my apron. "This is a surprise."

"Maeve, dear." Her smile was warm, but her eyes glinted cool blue. "I hope I'm not interrupting."

"Just potting seedlings." I gestured at the mess on my workbench. "What can I help you with?"

Alec's grandmother moved through my nursery with the careful deliberation of someone who preferred not to touch anything, though her eyes took in every detail. For a woman in her seventies, she moved with remarkable grace, her spine straight as a ruler.

"I'm looking for lavender." She paused to inspect a tray of herbs. "Ours isn't doing well this year."

I directed her to the lavender display, watching as she

selected a pot with particular care, holding it up to examine its roots through the drainage holes.

"How's the sawmill?" she asked casually, glancing over at me. "Derek tells me you've been a bit touchy lately. Threats to terminate his position. Talk of closing the mill."

"I wouldn't call them threats. More like—" I shrugged. "Considerations."

Betty set the lavender down and turned to face me, her smile fading. "The sawmill is a Lamb family asset. It has been for generations. It'd hate to see you drive it into the ground."

"The sawmill is mine now," I said quietly. "Legally and completely. What I do with it is my concern."

"Of course." Betty waved a hand dismissively. "But you have a responsibility to its legacy. To the town. To the Lamb name, which you carry."

"I carry my own name."

"You need to let Derek do his job, dear. So no more threats to sack him and close the mill, all right?"

She moved closer, and I caught a whiff of her perfume— attar of roses plus something darkly herbal. "And no more inter- ference with how he manages the property. Including the culling of those wild dogs. Let him have his fun."

My jaw clenched. Fun? I squared my shoulders. "Will that be all, Betty?"

She brought her lavender to the counter. "Derek said you've been seeing Fen Harkness."

My cheeks warmed, but I kept my voice steady. "He's a friend."

"We Lambs have avoided associating with Harkness clan for generations, and with good reason." She leaned forward slightly. "Fen Harkness is a loner. A law unto himself. Which makes him dangerous."

"You don't know him."

"I know how much Derek cares for you. I'd hate to see him get hurt. Like Alec."

She placed a crisp fifty-dollar note on the counter, far more than the lavender was worth. "Keep the change," she said. "Consider it goodwill between family."

The bell chimed as she left, and I stood there staring after her, hands trembling. It wasn't what Betty had said—it was how she'd said it. Like we were having two conversations at once, and I had only understood one of them.

15

───────

MAEVE

WHEN SATURDAY MORNING ROLLED AROUND, I wandered sleepily out to the front verandah with plates of fruit and seed for the wild birds that came every morning to feast. These past few days, Betty's visit had resurrected my old nightmares about Alec—for once, not his death in the forest—but the way he always made me feel like a naughty child on the brink of doing something wrong. The way I'd often walked on eggshells around him, too jumpy to relax.

I huffed out a breath. "He's gone, Maeve. And you rarely see his gran these days. Don't let the old battleaxe get under your skin, okay?"

As I was returning inside, I noticed the tartan picnic rug I had totally forgotten about—neatly folded, basking in a sunny spot on my bench seat. Freshly washed, with all the blood stains gone.

"Ah ... feeling better already."

On top of the rug sat a thin silver chain. When I picked it up, a scrap of paper fluttered beneath it, a message scrawled in strong, angular writing.

Thank you for saving me.

The chain caught the sunlight, a tiny silver owl spinning gently from it—reminding me of the beautiful boobook at Fen's place. My heart did a funny little skip.

"How gorgeous!"

As I slipped it over my head, a warm sensation enveloped me. I bit my lip, smiling crookedly as I recalled how gruff and ungrateful he'd seemed the night I stitched his wounds—at least until he took me out to meet the owl. He'd changed almost instantly then, as if the owl's presence had mellowed his sharp edges.

I stroked the silver charm with my thumb.

"Why Fen Harkness, you're a big ole cinnamon roll."

I returned inside still smiling, and before I could talk myself out of it, I was packing a picnic basket, tucking in the bottle of wine I'd been saving for a special occasion.

I arrived at the gothic mansion on Whitefeather Road mid-morning, the sun riding high over the distant hills. Fen's front window had been repaired, but the place looked deserted. I parked on the verge and walked around the back.

When I saw him cleaning out the cage with the boobook sitting serenely on the verandah rail nearby, I stopped in my tracks. Of course a vet would be great with animals, but there was something uncanny about how relaxed the bird was, her head bowed as she intently watched Fen work, her round eyes tracking his every move.

Suddenly, she turned towards me and let out a mewling sound.

Fen looked up. "Maeve."

"I got us some lunch." I touched the owl pendant hanging around my neck. "To say thank you."

A slow smile lit up his face. He slid on a falconry glove and extended his arm, inviting the owl to perch. Then he waved me over.

"Come and say hello."

The bird watched me climb the steps, her eyes glittering darkly in the morning light, snapping her beak as if to remind me how sharp it was. As I reached out my hand, she gave a mournful call and settled.

Her feathers were baby-soft under my fingers, yet I could feel her strength, too. When Fen replaced her in the clean cage, she hooted loudly, fluffing herself up.

"She likes you," Fen said.

"She's beautiful." I peered through the bars, shuffling closer. "But I thought you said she was wild?"

"She is."

"Why's she so tame? I'm kind of blown away that she let me pat her."

Fen looked pleased, but he didn't answer my question. He latched the cage and then turned to face me, eyeing the chain around my neck. He gave a lopsided grin, scraping his fingers through the dark stubble on his angular jaw.

"Suits you."

"How did you know I'd love it?"

"From the way your face lit up the other night when you saw our feathery friend here. She's nearly ready to release, I wanted you to remember her."

A rush of something warm and cosy flooded my limbs and I swayed towards him. I barely knew Fen, yet as I looked into his eyes I sensed that maybe I did know him after all. Not from the animal hospital, but from somewhere else, further back in time...

I gasped softly and stepped away, flushing at my crazy thoughts.

"You got anything planned today?" I said briskly, planting my hands on my hips to stop them from reaching for him.

He smiled slowly, his gaze locked on mine, his eyes darkening. I was sure they'd been green, but now they seemed almost grey—and vaguely predatory.

"I'm all yours."

I gulped, heatwaves rippling under my skin. My clothes seemed suddenly too tight, my neck burning as I struggled to break eye contact. I was like a drowning woman, only drowning in a sea of liquid heat. I flapped my hand in the general direction of the basket I'd brought.

"Picnic?"

His soft laugh sounded like a growl. "I know the perfect spot."

16

MAEVE

WE HIKED along the river near his house, the water babbling over rocks as the breeze sang through the casuarina trees. Pine scented the air, mingling with the earthy sweetness of warming soil.

"Here." Fen spread the old blanket he'd brought on a grassy bank overlooking the river. "Best view in Riverwood."

The water sparkled in the midday sun, leaves dancing overhead in patterns of light and shadow. Fen stretched out beside me, all lean muscle and quiet grace. I found myself studying the curve of his jaw, the way his dark hair fell across his forehead into his eyes, how his muscular shoulders moved beneath his shirt.

His eyes met mine, a faint smile curving his lips. "I can feel you watching me."

Heat crept up my throat. "Just trying to figure you out." I poured us both a glass of wine, grateful for the distraction. "The mysterious Fen Harkness."

"Not much to figure out." He took a sip, his gaze sliding away towards the river. "What you see is what you get."

"Somehow I doubt that." I pulled out containers of food—fresh bread, cheese, the strawberries I'd splurged on at the markets. "You know all about me. My past, my fears. But you never say much about yourself."

He was quiet for a long moment, watching the river flow past. "Some stories aren't worth telling."

"All stories are worth telling." I touched his arm lightly, feeling the warmth of his skin through his sleeve. "Even the difficult ones."

The muscle in his jaw tightened, but then he sighed.

"I guess you've heard the rumours. How my parents were killed in a hunting accident."

I nodded. "I'm sorry."

"Mum was brilliant, with a fierce heart. She found her match in my father. Soulmates. But loving him too much was probably her downfall."

"Why do you say that?"

"She would have survived that night if she hadn't gone back for him. He was badly wounded, and she died trying to save him."

I put down my sandwich, dusting off the crumbs as I looked at him. "Of course she went back. She would have been shattered to see him hurt."

"Like you were after Alec?"

I dropped my gaze. Nothing like Alec, though how could I admit that without sounding callous? So I just scraped my thumbnail over a dirt smudge on my jeans, saying nothing.

Fen huffed softly, then shifted closer. The movement was casual, but my bones hummed a little at his nearness. He swiped a lock of dark hair behind his ear.

"You and Mum would have gotten along." His voice grew softer. "She was a keen gardener, could grow anything. Her garden always seemed to be brimming over with flowers, even in winter—not to mention pretty much every vegetable known to humankind."

"I like her already."

"She had this long hair down to her waist." He chuckled softly, his eyes bright as they found me again. "My sister and I used to fight over whose turn it was to brush it for her. Little idiots we were. Just to get Mum's attention for a few minutes. God, we loved her."

"What happened to your sister?"

"Erin ran away. I guess the pressure of raising a kid brother got too much for her. I spent years searching, but she didn't want to be found."

"I'm sorry." I leaned over and threaded my fingers through his.

He squeezed back gently. "It was a long time ago."

"Still sucks though, doesn't it?"

His thumb traced circles on my hand, sending shivers up my arm. "Yeah. Still sucks."

We sat in silence, sharing food and wine as the afternoon mellowed around us. Despite what Derek and Nan had said about Fen being trouble, I felt safe with him. Seen. Maybe even understood.

I thought of the boy he'd once been, sweating in the stable yards, he and his sister trying to cope after their parents passed. Erin becoming unstable, Fen keeping his feelings buried. Had that made him into the guarded man he was now? Had his sister's grief turned him against love?

As if hearing my thoughts, he glanced over.

My breath caught.

His dark hair fell across the shadowed side of his face, the sunlight catching one eye and turning it silver. How could that be? I wanted to say it was a trick of the light, but with Fen there were so many mysteries that didn't add up. The way his injuries had healed so fast. The way the sunlight sometimes silvered his eyes. The way his gaze burned whenever he looked at me, but the moment I started getting to know him, his barricades slammed back up.

"Tell me something good," I said finally. "A happy memory."

His face softened into a smile, and something in my chest ached at the sight. "I used to camp out here as a kid. Spent hours watching the birds, learning their calls." He pointed to a flash of blue above us. "See that? Azure kingfisher. They mate for life, did you know?"

"Romantic little things, aren't they?"

"Nature often is," he remarked, his eyes darkening with an intensity that made my skin prickle. "Raw, honest, and without pretence."

I leaned in, drawn to the fierce energy radiating from him, as though he was one of the wild creatures he described.

"Is that why you prefer animals to people?"

"Partly." His voice dropped lower, rough around the edges, his gaze holding mine. "Though lately, I'm reconsidering my stance on humans."

My pulse quickened, little shivers flying over my skin. If I just moved a little closer...

Fen pulled back, breaking eye contact. He climbed to his feet and stretched, his gaze roaming into the trees. "We should head back. It's getting late."

I watched him pack up the remains of our picnic, his movements quick and efficient now, the moment of openness gone. Every time I thought I was getting closer to knowing him, he retreated behind those walls of his. And despite everything—despite Nan's warnings, and Derek's threats, and my own tangled feelings—I wanted to understand why.

17

MAEVE

WE HIKED BACK the way we'd come, then veered along a narrower trail. Fen called it a shortcut, but it took us further into the heart of the forest. The bush crackled with shadows and sounds. Bird calls, the rustling of grass. Unseen shapes darting beneath the towering trees.

Suddenly my cotton tank was damp and clingy.

"Is something following us?" I asked in a small voice, hating how scared I sounded.

Fen reached for my hand and moved between me and the shadowy trees, his shoulders squaring as his large fingers closed protectively around mine.

"I won't let anything hurt you, Maeve. I promise."

His voice carried more certainty than the situation needed, but I was grateful for his words. His skin was pleasantly rough, his fingers warm. I gripped them like a lifeline.

And just like that, my fears vanished.

I gaped at him. "How do you do that?" His hair had fallen forward over his face, and his bony nose reminded me of a hawk, but I'd never seen anyone looking more fierce. Or more beautiful. "First the owl, and now me."

"I'm a vet, remember," he said with a grin, the sharpness easing from his face as a strand of dark hair danced against his cheek in the warm breeze. "It's my job to make all my little creatures feel safe."

"I'm one of your little creatures?"

I expected him to deny it, to realise his blunder and backtrack, maybe even apologise, but his smile only widened, that possessive look coming back into his eyes.

"Only if you want to be."

My lips parted, and twin suns began to flame in my cheeks, sending heat right through my body. He swayed closer, his green gaze—or was it silver?—devouring me in a glance.

"You feel it too, don't you?" He spoke so softly, his words seeming to float from a dream, drifting around me like a spell. "I can see it in your eyes."

I wanted to pretend I had no idea what he was saying, or even what he meant. After all, I'd only known him for little over a week. Yet I found myself nodding, tiny switches flicking on in the back of my mind, like waking up, lighting up. Remembering.

"I feel it."

His gaze dropped to my lips, his tongue darting to the corner of his mouth, his nostrils flaring as he inhaled the sweet air.

"Good."

His grip tightened momentarily on my hand, and then he tugged me forward along the trail, but I dug in my heels.

"Fen, wait."

He looked back.

I blew a nervous breath. "I don't get it. We hardly know each other. But you're right, we have a connection. Why?"

His smile was slow, wistful. "Why does the moon affect people as well as the tides? Why do stars shine so brightly some nights, then others not at all?"

"Gravity? Atmospheric pollution?"

He nodded. "Science has all sorts of names for it. My mum was a scientist who branched into astronomy, studying lunar forces. Do you know what she called it?"

"What?"

"Magic."

He released my hand and kept walking, and I trailed close behind him, skipping along the narrow track and breathing in big gulps of the sweet, damp air.

Nan said Emeric and Evelina Harkness died in a hunting accident, which Fen's sister blamed on a family curse. A curse she'd become so obsessed with that it drove her off the rails. I couldn't ask Fen about the curse, because then he'd know I'd been snooping.

But all of a sudden I needed to know everything about him —his present, his past. His clash with the Lambs. His family and the secrets hanging over them. Everything.

Because it was clear I was fast developing an obsession of my own—and not with some made-up family curse.

18

———————

FEN

WE REACHED the house as the sun was sinking, our bellies grumbling despite the picnic. While I made pasta with tomatoes and basil from the garden, Maeve assembled a salad.

Afterwards, we lounged on the front verandah to watch the sunset over the mountains. Finishing the wine, cicadas chirping around us as the sky blushed deep pink. Maeve lay back on the cushions, her hair the colour of autumn leaves, her cheeks flushed after our day in the forest.

"Alec and I were opposites." Her voice was thoughtful as she went through the motion of twisting a wedding ring that wasn't there. "People said it was a good thing, but I'm not so sure. A naturalist and a sawmill operator, oil and water."

"I guess you never truly know anyone."

She turned her amber gaze on me. "Sounds like there are ghosts in your past, too?"

Too many. "Nothing interesting."

"See, there you go again." She propped herself up on one elbow, studying my face. "Every time I ask about you, you shut down. Why is that?"

Because I'm the monster from your nightmares. Because I'm falling for you and I can't seem to stop. Because the wolf in me has already claimed you as his mate, and the man in me is terrified of hurting you.

"Just private, I guess."

She huffed out a breath, blowing a strand of hair from her face. "Fine. Keep your secrets, Fen Harkness. But someday I'll figure you out."

God, I hoped not. But I couldn't help smiling at her determination. "That a threat?"

"A promise." She sat up and leaned over so we were almost touching. My nostrils flared. I could smell the sunshine on her skin and see the tiny freckles dusting her nose. She smiled. "I'm getting pretty good at solving puzzles these days."

"Is that what I am? A puzzle?"

Her gaze dropped to my mouth, then back up. "Among other things."

The wolf surged forward, hungry for her, and I found myself leaning in. She swayed closer, her lips parting slightly, and for one burning moment I imagined closing the distance. Tasting her. Claiming her.

The breeze shifted, bringing her scent around me, stirring the shadows in my soul.

"I should feed the owl," I managed, pushing to my feet, hating how lame it sounded. "Want to help me release her next weekend?"

"Thought you'd never ask." Her smile was a little unsteady, but genuine. "As long as you promise not to run away again."

If only she knew how impossible that was becoming. I was in too deep to leave her alone, even though I should. Even though loving me could destroy her. Just as love had destroyed my family.

"Next weekend then." I helped her up, careful not to let my touch linger. "Promise."

19

MAEVE

THE FOLLOWING MORNING, I woke feeling braver than I had in years. Our picnic had been so perfect that my veins still hummed with pleasure. Who'd have thought that a day in the forest could bring two people so close together? There was still so much about Fen I didn't know, but I was now optimistic it was just a matter of time.

Wanting to test out my new courage, I laced on my hiking boots and drove out to one of my old favourite trails, just north of the sawmill.

Along with the mill, I'd inherited the thousand hectares of bushland it sat on. Much of the land had been cleared, but two years ago I'd started replanting some of the bare areas with seeds I'd collected there.

I could walk over now and see how many had survived.

The old logging trail wound through stands of spotted gum, dappled sunlight playing across the leaf-littered path. After spending yesterday by the river with Fen, everything felt different. The sounds that used to terrify me—creaking branches, rustling leaves, the cry of a distant crow—now felt like old friends.

I smiled to myself. Fen. What a mystery he was turning out to be. Sweet one moment. The next, on fire.

I'm one of your little creatures?

Only if you want to be.

Something moved in the undergrowth behind me. Instead of panic, a strange calm settled over me. I knew who it was.

"Following me again?" I murmured, but when I turned, the trail was empty.

The path curved ahead and as I climbed a low hill, the metallic clink of tools drifted to me. My heart sank when I saw him. Derek knelt in the dirt a little way off the track, his ute parked behind him at the edge of an extensive cleared area. He was hammering a rod stake into the ground to secure another of his cruel traps.

He looked up at my approach, his face splitting into a familiar smug smile. "Well, if it isn't little Mae-Mae, out for a walk all alone."

I touched the owl pendant at my throat, drawing strength from it. "Those traps are illegal, Derek."

"Going to report me?" He rose, brushing dirt from his knees and stalked over. As his gaze travelled over me, his eyes caught on the necklace, narrowing. "That's new. Gift from the vet?"

I took a step back. "None of your business."

"Didn't think he was your type." Derek's hand shot out, grabbing the pendant. "But then, you always did like dangerous men."

"Let go!" I shoved him hard, but he caught my wrists, yanking me against him.

"Come on, Mae." His breath was hot on my face, reeking of

tobacco. "You know you belong with me. I'm the only one who really knows you. Let's have a little fun, eh?

"You want the mill," I said through clenched teeth. "You were always jealous that Alec got it and not you. So stop pretending it's me you want."

"That's where you're wrong, Maeve. Why can't a man have it all?" His voice dripped with arrogance as he shoved me against the rough bark of a tree trunk. His other hand fisted in my blouse, tearing the light fabric.

"Get off me!" I shouted, struggling to push him away, but his grip was unyielding, and his face loomed closer, his mouth coming down—

A snarl ripped through the air.

The grey wolf burst from the shadows, massive and terrible, teeth bared. Derek stumbled back, releasing me. The wolf positioned itself between us, another growl rumbling deep in its chest.

"Bloody hell." Derek's hand went to his belt, but his knife wasn't there.

The wolf advanced, driving him further along the trail. But it didn't attack. It just stood there, its pale eyes fixed on Derek with deadly focus, its snarl rumbling.

Derek stumbled back, retreating towards the clearing. "I'm not done with you, Maeve. This isn't over."

I watched him turn and jog toward his ute, my whole body trembling. Only when the sound of his engine faded did I look around for the wolf.

But the trail was empty. My protector had vanished as silently as he'd appeared.

I touched my throat where the pendant still hung, then the torn edges of my blouse. The forest felt different again, but not with fear this time. Instead, a strange certainty settled over me.

I wasn't alone out here. Maybe I never had been.

20

MAEVE

FEN'S MOTORBIKE gleamed in the afternoon sun as he pulled into my driveway. It was Saturday, a week since our picnic by the river, and today we were releasing the boobook.

"Nice bike," I said, smoothing a damp palm on my embroidered vintage jeans. "Looks fast."

"Ever been on one?" He held out a helmet.

I shook my head, heart racing as I squashed the helmet over my springy hair and buckled the chin strap.

"They seemed a little dangerous. Always wanted to, though."

"Well then." His eyes crinkled at the corners. "Hop on."

The bike roared to life beneath us, and I wrapped my arms around Fen's waist, pressing close against the warm leather of his jacket. We followed the river road, its endless bends carrying us away from town and deeper into the forest. Wind whipped at my clothes, and as we slowed to take a curve, I reached up without thinking and slipped off the helmet.

"Mae!" Fen's voice carried back to me. "What the heck?"

I laughed, letting my hair stream behind me. After my close encounter in the forest with Derek—and the grey wolf—something strange had happened. I felt different. As if I'd been trapped in a bad dream for the past two years, and now, with the forest flashing past in a blur of green and gold, I was absolutely, perfectly awake.

"I'm alive!" I shouted, then let out a squeal.

I felt Fen's chuckle more than heard it, vibrating through his back against my chest.

The roar of the motorbike echoed through the trees as we sped down the winding forest road, the canopy of leaves flickering green shadows around us. With each mile, the weight of the past seemed lighter, unravelling with every gust of crisp, piney air that hit my face. As the setting sun painted the landscape gold, turning the river beside us into a shimmering copper ribbon, my fingers unclenched from Fen's jacket and I rested against him with an ease I'd never known. I'd spent so long walking the safe paths, keeping to the familiar, that I'd forgotten how it felt to simply *move*—to let the world rush past without counting every careful step.

We arrived back at Fen's as the sun skimmed the horizon, shadows gathering under the gum trees in his garden.

On the verandah, the boobook watched us solemnly while Fen checked its wing. Behind him on the wall hung a collection of vintage garden tools—secateurs, pruning saws, trowels, a rusty sickle—which I'd seen before, but the golden light picked out every gorgeous, rusty detail. Hidden among them, a small, ornate double-edged dagger, barely longer than my hand. I drifted closer. Its silver blade was etched with strange symbols, its polished wooden hilt intricately carved.

"Beautiful, isn't it?" Fen's voice was carefully neutral. "Family heirloom."

"Some kind of knife?"

"It's called an athame. A ceremonial dagger."

"Those markings…" I stepped nearer, drawn by the inscription on the blade, my fingers itching to touch. "What's written there, can I see?"

Fen hovered protectively, crowding me a little as he unhooked it from the wall and walked over to the light, gripping the hilt. "It's sharp. Be careful."

I leaned against his arm, squinting at the blade and the swirling longhand words inscribed on it. "This curse I take, from thee—" Before I could read the rest, Fen flipped it over. There was more writing on the blade, a language I didn't recognise. Around the script was a flourish of leaves and flowers with a tiny wolf at the heart.

"Family legend says it carries a curse," he said, his voice low and husky.

So Nan was right, there was a Harkness curse. And the way Fen was frowning at the knife right now, holding it so awkwardly, unsettled me a little. He didn't believe it. Did he?

"What sort of curse?"

He inhaled slowly, his eyes darting to me, then back to the athame. "Pretty dramatic stuff—madness, tragedy, that sort of thing."

"But curses can be broken, right?" I smiled, hoping to lighten him up, but his frown only deepened.

"Not this one. At least…" His shoulders twitched, and he finally met my eyes. "Not without a sacrifice."

"That sounds dark. Why do you keep it on display?"

"I'm out here all the time in summer." He waved a hand at the Bali lounge with its comfy cushions and the redwood dining table and chairs beside it. "I eat outside. Spend hours reading. Sometimes, I even crash here for the night. The athame reminds me what I have to be grateful for."

"What's that?"

"My parents sacrificed a lot for me and my sister Erin. In a way, they gave their lives protecting us. There's no greater love than that."

"Protecting you from what?"

He blew out a breath. "Riverwood has some pretty shady things going on. Not everything—or everyone—here is what they seem."

I frowned, shaking my head. "You'd get along well with my nan. She said the same thing the other day."

"Your nan's a wise woman."

"But you don't really believe your family is cursed, do you?"

"Course not." But his laugh was hollow. "Though it would explain a few things. Like why I've always been unlucky in love."

"Then I'm cursed, too." I'd meant it lightly, but my smile quickly faded when Fen turned abruptly and replaced the knife on the wall.

"I guess some people just aren't meant for happy endings," he said so quietly I almost missed it.

Tension rippled across his shoulders as he went back to the owl's cage. His hands trembled slightly as he stretched the bird's injured wing, feeling gently along the delicate bones.

He wasn't joking about the curse.

He truly believed it.

I watched the way he handled the little bird of prey with a mix of confidence and care—this mysterious man who rescued injured animals, even the wolves that everyone else despised. But *cursed*?

It seemed so farfetched.

In the short time I'd known him, Fen had done what no one else had been able to do. He'd stepped in between me and my fears, giving me the courage to finally confront them. He was hilarious and charming, not to mention pretty damn easy on the eyes. How could he possibly think he was cursed to be unlucky in love? And more importantly, how could I convince him otherwise?

21

———————

MAEVE

THE BOOBOOK'S powerful talons gripped Fen's gloved forearm, its feathers rippling in the breeze. We stood in a grassy clearing on the edge of the forest, the empty cage beside us, late afternoon sunlight streaming through the canopy.

"Ready?" Fen murmured.

I nodded, hardly daring to breathe. He lifted his arm, and the owl launched skyward, her wings spreading wide. Fen unbuckled the falconry glove as we watched her soar into the treetops, her shadow dancing across the forest floor.

"She's flying!" I grabbed Fen's hand as the owl banked and flew further into the forest. I tugged him forward. "Come on, let's follow her!"

We chased the owl's shadow deeper into the trees, ducking under branches and leaping over fallen logs. I couldn't remember the last time I'd felt so free. So fearless. The forest that had haunted my nightmares was now starting to feel safe again.

As the owl disappeared into the canopy, we emerged into a sun-drenched hollow carpeted with tiny purple wildflowers. I spun in a circle, laughing, until my foot caught on a root. Fen caught me as I stumbled, and we both went down, rolling in the flowers.

"You're crazy," he said, but he was laughing too, flower petals caught in his dark hair.

"Maybe." I reached up to brush them away, my fingers lingering against his cheek. "But at least I'm not cursed."

His smile faded, but he didn't pull away. Not this time. Instead, he leaned closer, one hand coming up to cradle my face, his thumb tracing across my chin.

"Better crazy than cursed," he breathed. "I'd hate to forget you."

"Huh. No chance of that. I'll make sure of it."

"Promise?"

I leaned into his palm, the rough calluses a tantalising contrast against his warm skin. "So this curse makes you forget?"

"Only if it's broken."

I wanted to pull away from him, laugh a little, feeling strangely uneasy. Were we joking right now, or was this a red flag? Warning me that maybe Fen, like his sister, had the potential for going off the rails?

"Then let's not break it," I whispered. "Ever."

Fen frowned suddenly, glancing away into the trees. When he looked back, a stray sunbeam caught his eyes and his irises briefly flared silver.

My breath caught.

Something rippled at the back of my mind, a glimpse of silvery white flashing in the firelight, a fragment from a forgotten dream. Or a memory—

Before I could fully process what was happening, Fen moved in a fluid motion, trapping me between his elbows, his big warm body laying hard across the length of mine. His sudden closeness lit a fire in me. My heart ran wild, a demented drumbeat in my chest and throat as I lost myself in the green depths of his gaze.

"Maeve," he whispered. "Stay very still."

He needn't have worried. My limbs had turned to molten jelly, I wasn't going anywhere. Drowning and helpless in those icy pale green pools, almost convinced that he was right about the curse because how could a stolen moment like this feel so right—and so terrifying, all at the same time? Maybe I was crazy, but right now, as the soft sunlight danced with the forest shadows around us, there was just us and nothing else mattered.

"Fen..."

He lowered his mouth towards mine, and I raised my lips eagerly to meet his—

A low growl froze us both.

We sprang apart. At the edge of the hollow stood a black wolf, massive and terrible, its dark fur bristling.

Every muscle in my body, languid and at ease just a moment before, was now rigid and frozen, caught in an almost painful grip of tension. This wolf was nothing like my grey one. Nothing about its energy was protective, or calm. Rather, its large body radiated aggression.

I swallowed a whimper.

It was happening again.

The campfire embers, the night forest silent except for Alec's cries and the savage snarls of the beast that was killing him—

Only this time around I wasn't arguing, and I wasn't with a man I secretly detested, but with one I was starting to like very much. Maybe even to love. I wanted to shut my eyes, but that would only bring it all crashing back—Alec's scream, his blood spurting on the leaves, death swallowing the darkness. And the wolf. The shadow-wolf who killed him.

So I kept my eyes wide, unable to breathe as I stared at the monster now facing us.

Fen was already on his feet, positioning himself between me and the wolf.

And then he did something incredible. He looked directly into the wolf's eyes, holding its gaze. The wolf's growl deepened, but Fen didn't flinch. He just stood there, calm as could be, as if he was having a silent conversation with the creature.

After what felt like forever, he reached back for my hand. "Come on. Nice and slow."

"Fen—"

"I won't let anything happen to you, Maeve." His voice was steady, certain. "Trust me."

I climbed to my feet and we backed away carefully, the wolf watching our every move. I couldn't seem to get a grip on myself, trembling all over, my legs lurching woodenly along the trail, my palm slick with sweat as I clung to Fen's fingers like a frightened child.

Only when we were out of the hollow did Fen turn us toward the sunny clearing where we released the owl, his hand warm and sure around mine.

I was still trembling. "What if it follows?"

"It won't."

"But it might."

"He won't hurt us," he said calmly.

"You don't know that."

"Yeah, Mae. I do."

"How, though?"

"I'm a vet. I'm trained to know about wild things."

"Really?"

"Just look back, is he following us?"

Reluctantly, I turned my head, my sweaty fingers still gripping his. He was right. Between the trees, the wolf stood motionless, its muzzle relaxed now. Only its dark gaze followed, tracking our every move with a ravenous glint.

As we walked, Fen's calm energy wrapped around me, and my jitters began to fade. I glanced back again, but the wolf had gone.

In its place, though, a terrible thought bloomed. What if Fen wasn't joking about the curse? What if everything—his family legend, the cursed athame, and his belief in dark forces—was real?

But then he squeezed my hand, and I pushed the thoughts away. Curse or no curse, I wasn't giving up on him. Not when I was finally starting to feel like myself again.

22

MAEVE

The following Saturday afternoon, I drove out to
Whitefeather Road, parking on the verge in front of Fen's
house. Fen was out the back watering his veggie patch, and
when he saw me he shut off the hose and strode over.

"Hey, stranger."

"I've got a surprise for you," I said, bouncing on my toes,
unable to contain my excitement. "You showed me something
special last weekend. Now it's my turn."

His brow quirked up. "Where are we heading today?"

"Get your hiking boots on. I want to show you my favourite
place in the whole forest."

I hopped from foot to foot while he laced up and then he
grabbed my hand, tugging me towards his bike.

"Keep your damn helmet on this time, okay?"

I laughed, punching him playfully on the arm. "We'll see,
granny."

Sunlight slanted through the trees, painting everything
golden as we hiked deeper into the bush. Fen's fingers were
warm around mine, his thumb stroking absent patterns against

my skin. With him beside me, everything felt different—the forest, the shadows that swarmed around the tree trunks, the whippy saplings that grew in patches of light. The bush was no longer a place of fear for me but a magical place shimmering with sunlight, warmth, and possibility—

"Watch your step." Fen pulled me to a halt, crouching to examine something half-hidden in the leaves. A steel trap, its savage teeth waiting to snap shut.

"Looks like someone's hell-bent on causing chaos." Fen's voice was tight as he carefully disabled the mechanism. When he stood up, his eyes were guarded and his jaw clenched. "Your brother-in-law is so obsessed with getting revenge that he doesn't even notice the damage he's doing to other wildlife. Like our boobook friend."

"I don't think he cares."

"Wild places aren't just for us humans, they're for all creatures."

"I think Derek just likes killing things."

Fen absently rubbed his forearm where there was still the faint trace of a pink scar. "Maybe if he replanted some of the bushland he's cleared or just left more places for the critters to hide away, tragic accidents like Alec's death might not happen."

I studied the trap. A buildup of grime and old blood blackened its jaws. Bush flies buzzed over the sausage chunks scattered around it as bait.

"I get why he hates the wolves," I said softly. "For a long time, I hated them too."

"You were scared of them, Maeve. There's a difference."

"Thanks to you, I'm learning to respect them. Maybe even like them a little."

His brow shot up. "Like them?"

"I didn't tell you this, but a few weeks ago, my grey wolf saved me."

"*Your* grey wolf?"

I nodded, pushing a strand of damp hair back off my face. "I went for a hike in the forest and ran into Derek. He started being an arse, and the wolf sprang out and chased him off."

"You went hiking without me?"

"I wanted to see if I was brave enough. And aside from the Derek incident, I rocked it."

Fen's lips softened into a half-smile. "You're amazing, you know that?"

"Come on," I said, trying not to smile too widely as I slid my fingers into his, tugging him forward along the path. "We're almost there. Just wait till you see this tree. It's a giant spotted gum, must be centuries old. It has these big woody pods, and I've collected a ton of seeds from it over the years."

"How did you discover it?"

"Nan took me and Kitty there ages ago. There's some scarring at the base where Nan thinks the First Nations people cut away bark to make their coolamons and shields. After that, I hiked out here a lot with friends or by myself. It's really special."

As we got closer, something didn't feel right. Usually, this part of the forest was always dark because the old spotted gum blocked out the light. But today, it seemed brighter. There was way too much sunlight pouring onto the trail in a place that was supposed to be dim and cool.

When I noticed the tyre tracks carving deep ruts in the earth, and wood splinters littering the ground, I broke away from Fen and raced ahead.

"No!" My steps slowed. "Oh, no."

Where my beautiful tree had stood, there was only a massive stump, its rings exposed to the sky like an open wound. The great trunk lay broken and butchered on the ground, its branches hacked away, the shattered limbs of other trees crushed beneath it.

A cry tore from my throat. I stumbled forward, falling to my knees beside the stump. My fingers traced the fresh saw marks, coming away sticky with sap.

"Mae." Fen's arms wrapped around me from behind, pulling me against his chest as I began to shake. "I'm so sorry."

"He did this to punish me." My voice cracked. "Derek did this. For saving that wolf at the mill. For rejecting his slimy advances. Because his brother left the sawmill to me instead of him."

Fen's arms tightened around me. "Those bloody Lambs, acting like they run this town. They're trouble, Mae. Promise me you won't try to fight back, all right?"

I nodded against his shoulder, but all I could see was Derek's mocking smile, hear his threats. The tree had been here longer than any of us, had weathered storms and fires. The deep woods had been a sacred place long before white settlers arrived, the spotted gum one of its oldest guardians. And Derek had destroyed it just to hurt me.

I turned in Fen's arms, pressing my tear-streaked face against his neck. Breathing the comforting scent of his skin, the warm pine and woodsmoke drifting off his shirt. His pulse beat strong and steady against my cheek, his hands gentle as they stroked my back. But beneath the gentleness, I sensed something fierce and protective—something that understood exactly how I felt.

"I want to make him pay," I whispered.

Fen's hands stilled, and he pressed his lips to my hair. "Mae, listen to me. The Lambs are not what they seem—they're way more powerful than anyone knows. Revenge will only make things worse. Not just for you but for your family. Trust me, I know."

I pulled back to look at him. There was something in his eyes—a shadow of old pain, of secrets kept too long. But before

I could ask, he cupped my face in his hands, thumbs brushing away my tears.

"Let me take you home," he murmured.

I cast one last look at my murdered tree. The forest felt darker now, wounded. Broken. Or maybe that was just my heart.

But as Fen helped me to my feet, holding me close as we walked back through the gathering shadows, I knew one thing for certain—I was done letting Derek Lamb hurt the things I loved. I would find a way to make him pay for destroying this place. It might not be tomorrow, or the next day, or even the day after that.

Yet his time would come.

The Lambs might be powerful—but the Winters clan was patient. Nan had taught me that. I would watch and wait, even if it took years—and when the perfect time arrived, I would strike.

23

MAEVE

Fen parked in my driveway, and then walked me to my door. "Sure you're okay, Maeve?"

I shook my head. My face felt puffy, and I probably had raccoon eyes after crying against his back for the whole ride home.

"I can't bear the thought of being alone tonight." Not after finding my beautiful spotted gum reduced to a scarred stump, its rings exposed like an open weeping wound. Knowing Derek had cut it down because of me was more than I felt able to cope with right now. "Will you stay?"

His eyes locked onto mine. "You sure about this?"

I nodded. Since finding the tree, Fen's gaze had hardly strayed from me. He had held my hand the whole way back to the parking area, his fingers curled protectively around mine, his warmth shielding me from the icy chill in my heart.

"More than anything."

Inside, I busied myself opening windows to let in the evening breeze while Fen found wine glasses, leaning against the kitchen counter to uncork the bottle, watching me with a quiet intensity that made my skin tingle.

"Make yourself comfortable," I said, gesturing toward the deck. "I'll bring out some snacks."

I made a tray of sourdough sandwiches and other nibblies and then went around lighting the colourful Moroccan lanterns hanging from the verandah rafters. They cast a warm, golden glow that caught in the climbing jasmine and softened the gathering dusk. Fen had settled onto the oversized daybed I'd dragged outside months ago, where I'd been retreating to after work to read.

I set a portable speaker on the small side table and scrolled through my phone until I found something suitably mellow—low, sultry jazz that seemed to melt into the evening air.

"Nice place," Fen said, passing me a glass of wine. "It suits you."

"Oh?"

"Cosy. Welcoming." His mouth curved into his trademark half-smile that always made my heart skip. "A little wild around the edges."

I laughed, curling up beside him on the daybed, sipping my wine. "You think I'm wild?"

"I think you'd like to be."

"I always feel a bit crazy and free on the back of your bike. "

"I can tell."

I shook my head, laughing a little as I relived the moment I'd taken off my helmet that first time, feeling the wind whip my hair behind me, the green scent of the forest pulsing around us. "Nan always warned me about straying off the path. She said girls who stray come to a bad end. But I've always dreamed of something more, you know?"

"Something beyond the path?"

"Being fearless, not caring what others think. At peace with who I am."

He studied me, his eyes faintly silver in the lantern light. "You're not at peace now?"

"Not even close. And after seeing my poor ruined tree, I'm not sure it's even possible anymore."

"It's definitely possible. I bet you'll find it all one day. Everything you're looking for. And when that happens, you'll return to the spotted gum, plant those seeds you collected, and start a brand new cycle of life."

"You make it sound so epic."

"It is epic. Once you embrace who you are and let everything else go, your life will change in big ways."

"Good ways, I hope."

"The best."

I took another gulp of wine. "Do you think it's true, Fen? That people who stray from the normal path and blaze their own trail end up destroying their lives?"

He put his glass down and scooted closer, linking his fingers through mine. "I reckon it's the other way around. Only those who carve out their own path truly get to live."

"I wish I was as brave as you."

He smiled, and little dimples appeared that I hadn't noticed before, or maybe I had, but they'd never charmed me as much as they did right now.

"You have courage, Maeve." He said softly. "Hey, you went hiking alone near the sawmill the other day, didn't you?"

"Yeah." My smile faltered. "I never told you I was near the mill."

His dimples vanished. "Huh, maybe I'm psychic."

"You didn't follow me out there too, did you?"

"Only in my dreams."

I rolled my eyes and flopped back into the plush cushions,

my shoulder relaxed against his. We watched the sun sink lower, painting the sky in strokes of amber and rose. The first stars were just beginning to appear when Fen's attention shifted to the eastern horizon.

"Moon's rising," he said.

I followed his gaze to where the pale silver orb was climbing above the treeline. "Nearly full."

"Three days." His voice had roughened, and when I looked over, his profile was sharp against the darkness, jaw tight.

"Does it bother you? The moon?"

He took a long swallow of wine before answering. "My family always had a complicated relationship with the moon."

"Because of the curse?"

His eyes flicked to mine, then away. "My mum used to say that because of the curse, the moon was both our worst enemy —and our closest friend. When it's full, we change. Become something lost and broken. Shunned by the world. The only way we can find our way back to ourselves is by following the moon."

"Shunned? That's kind of heavy."

"Maeve, you don't know the half of it."

"Then tell me," I said softly. "Help me understand."

"Maybe I will someday. But not tonight, okay?" He shifted back to look at me, his smile somehow pained. "I know how it sounds. Curses, right? But some things are true whether you believe in them or not."

I considered his words, thinking of all the fears I'd let define me over the years. The monsters I'd let dominate my mind and fill me with fear, even after they were dead and buried.

"I suppose you're right," I admitted. "I believed marriage was forever. I believed someone who said they loved you wasn't supposed to hurt you. And I believed all wolves were dangerous. Until that grey one proved me wrong."

Something flickered in Fen's expression—relief, maybe, or hope. But then his gaze drifted back to the rising moon, and that familiar shadow passed over his features.

I couldn't bear to see him retreat behind his walls. Not tonight. Not right now when we were closer than we'd ever been before. I untangled my fingers and went over to the old cedar chest where I kept odds and ends for my shop displays.

"What are you doing?" Fen asked.

I pulled out a length of pink sequined fabric I'd used in last year's Easter window. "Brightening things up."

The silver spangles caught the lantern light as I wrapped it around my waist, letting it fall in a makeshift skirt over my jeans. Then I turned up the music and began to dance, swaying my hips seductively.

"Mae..." But he was already softening, the brooding look fading as I shimmied closer, sequins throwing tiny stars across his face.

"Come on, wolf man." I took his hands, pulling him toward me. "Live a little."

"Wolf man?"

"Well, technically wolf-whisperer, after the way you charmed that monster in the wildflower hollow. But it doesn't have the same ring."

I wiggled my eyebrows and spun, the sequins catching the lantern light and scattering it across the deck. Suddenly, he was laughing—a full, rich sound that sent pleasure tingling through my veins.

"You're ridiculous," he said, but his eyes flashed with something that made my breath catch.

"You love it."

"You're right," he growled, springing to his feet in one fluid movement. Before I could react, he caught me and scooped me up, one arm behind my knees, and the other around my back.

"Things are definitely brighter," he murmured, his lips close to my ear.

The sequinned cloth slipped to the deck as he carried me back to the daybed, my heart thumping wildly against my ribs. He laid me down gently, following me into the cushions until we were face to face, his weight supported on his forearms.

"Maeve," he whispered.

I answered by threading my fingers through his hair and pulling him down on me. The first touch of his lips was soft, questioning, but when I arched up against him, the kiss deepened, all the longing I didn't know I'd been holding onto poured out in the press of lips, the slide of tongues, the catch of teeth. His hands traced fire down my sides, thumbs brushing the undersides of my breasts through my shirt before settling at my hips.

I tugged at the hem of his shirt, suddenly desperate to feel his skin against mine.

Lantern light painted patterns across his tattooed shoulders as I helped him out of his shirt, and then mine followed, my fingers tracing the lean muscles of his chest.

"Mae," he breathed against my throat, and I arched into him. His touch was hungry as if, like me, he'd been starved of love too long.

The night air raised goosebumps on my exposed skin, but Fen's hands were warm as they explored.

"Are you sure?" he asked, voice ragged, as I reached for the button of his jeans.

"I've never been more sure of anything," I whispered back, and it was true. Whatever mysteries surrounded Fen, whatever secrets he still kept, I wanted this—wanted him—with a certainty that outweighed all my usual caution.

Piece by piece, our remaining clothes fell away, until there was nothing between us but skin and breath and the moonlit night. Fen took his time, his hands and mouth mapping every inch of me until I was trembling. When he finally sank into me, we both gasped. For a moment, we were perfectly still, foreheads pressed together, the moonlight bathing us in silver.

"I've wanted this since I first saw you," he breathed, his voice barely audible. "Even half-conscious on the forest road that night, I wanted you so much it scared me."

"Me too," I admitted. "Even when you were infuriating me."

He smiled against my lips, then began to move. We found our rhythm easily, as if we'd been lovers for years instead of moments. His eyes never left mine, even as the pleasure built between us, coiling tighter and tighter until it finally broke in a rush that left me gasping his name.

Afterwards, we lay tangled together beneath the light throw I kept on the daybed, watching the moon climb higher in the night sky. Fen's fingers traced patterns on my shoulder, and I nestled closer against his chest, listening to the steady beat of his heart.

"What are you thinking?" I tilted my head to see his face.

His smile was unguarded, almost boyish. "That I don't remember the last time I felt this ... peaceful."

I understood exactly what he meant. The hum of anxiety that had been my companion for so long had quieted to almost nothing in his arms. For the first time in years, I felt fully present, fully alive.

"I could get used to this," I murmured, not realising I'd spoken aloud until his arms tightened around me.

"So could I."

In the warm cocoon of the moment, I let myself imagine our future—mornings waking up beside him, evenings spent like this, sharing the quiet moments that make up a life together. Building something lasting and real. The vision was so clear, so achingly possible, that tears pricked behind my eyes. Maybe Nan was wrong about love being a curse. Maybe a happy ending was possible, after all?

I turned my face into his chest, suddenly overwhelmed by the intensity of my feelings for this complicated, guarded man.

"Hey," he said softly, tilting my chin up. "What is it?"

"Nothing. Just…" I swallowed past the tightness in my throat. "I'm happy."

He studied my face for a long moment, then cupped my cheek and murmured against my hair. "So am I." He hesitated, then added, "I didn't think I ever could be. Not like this."

The admission squeezed my heart. I pressed a kiss to his palm, then settled back against him, both of us falling silent as we watched the moon rise higher, bright and nearly full, illuminating the night with its silver glow.

Whatever happened next, whatever challenges we faced, tonight had changed everything. There was no going back to the careful distance we'd maintained before, no going back to our easy friendship. His talk about the curse and the moon's impact on his family, and how seriously he took it—that was all a part of him, and now it was a part of me, too.

And crazily enough, I wouldn't have had it any other way.

24

MAEVE

WHEN I WOKE in the morning, Fen was gone. I scrambled off the daybed, thinking he'd escaped home—but then the scent of toast and coffee reached me. Fen emerged onto the verandah carrying a breakfast tray.

"Hungry?"

I gave a little growl, my gaze travelling over his muscular body, lingering where the waist of his jeans rode low over his hips. "Starving. But not for toast."

"Steady, tiger. You need your energy."

He placed the tray on the deck beside the daybed and climbed in with me, his lingering kiss igniting me all over again. I smoothed my palms over his shoulders, my thumb tracing his tattoos. A flowering vine wound around his biceps, framing a fierce-looking wolf. Another wolf. He was certainly obsessed with them. The motifs seemed familiar, and it took a moment to remember where I'd seen them before.

I pulled back. "These designs are from the athame?"

"Hmm."

"You're serious about that curse, aren't you?"

"Have to be."

"Okay, so if we're going to..." I gestured behind me at the crumpled throws and pillows. "Keep doing *that*—which I really hope we are, by the way—then I'll need to know more about this curse of yours."

He was quiet for a long moment, then stood up, reaching into the pocket of his jeans and bringing out a small velvet pouch.

"I've been wanting to give you this."

Inside was a ring, delicately hand-crafted in silver. Tiny wolves ran around the wide band, chasing each other through miniature wildflowers. It was the most beautiful thing I'd ever seen.

"For protection," he said softly, sliding it onto my finger. "And to help you feel braver."

"It's perfect." I touched one of the tiny wolves. "But why do I need protection?"

"You asked about the curse."

"I was wondering when you'd get to that."

"I have to tell you something." His voice was rough, his eyes steady on mine. "About me. About what I am."

I held my breath, waiting. But whatever he was trying to say seemed stuck in his throat. Finally, he shook his head.

"You know, Maeve. Maybe I should go."

"Stay," I whispered. "I don't need to know about it, not if it makes you uncomfortable."

But he was already pulling away, the haunted look back in his eyes.

"I just don't want you to get hurt. I know how tough the last couple of years have been for you. The last thing I want is to cause you anymore grief."

"You won't ... Fen—?"

I watched him put on his boots and retrieve his shirt from

the end of the daybed, my heart sinking but not knowing how to make him stay. He paused in the doorway, looking back at me with such longing it made my heart hurt.

"Yesterday was fun," he murmured. "And last night..." He pulled away from the door and strode back over the deck, gathering me into a tight embrace, his lips capturing mine with the same fiery passion we had shared last night. "Being with you was incredible, you know? Even if I make it to a hundred, it'll still be the highlight of my life."

"Then spend the day with me. Stay again tonight."

He glanced out at the sky, a tiny frown creasing his brows as he followed some invisible trajectory across the horizon.

"My heart wants to stay. Forever, if you'd have me. But there'll be nights I have to be alone. Like tonight. Trust me, it's safer this way."

My heart dropped, not understanding, but wanting to with every fibre in my soul. I raised my hand, the silver ring catching the early light.

"But I am safe, right?"

"And you need to stay that way."

As his bike roared away into the morning, I touched the ring on my finger, tracing the tiny wildflowers and wolves with their forever love. Whatever Fen was afraid to tell me, whatever secrets he was keeping—it didn't matter. I was already his, whether he knew it or not.

Whether he was ready for it or not.

25

FEN

THE MOON DRIFTED large and full over Maeve's cottage, its powerful light casting shadows that writhed and leapt in the darkness of the quiet street below. Beside me, Maeve slept deeply, her hair coiling across the pillow, her breath soft against my arm.

I should leave.

Slip away now before the silvery moonlight reached inside me and forced me to change. Forced me to spend the night in the forest hunting and racing my shadow. Then having to avoid Maeve for days while the curse was most unpredictable—making excuses, even lying to her. Anything to keep her out of my violent, secret world.

This past month had sped by too quickly. Almost in a blur. Since that first night on the daybed, Maeve and I had been inseparable. Either I was here at her place, or she was hanging out at mine almost every night. If I thought I was obsessed with her before, now my feelings were off the charts. Being with her brought me back to life in ways I never imagined possible. I felt alive, seen. Loved. Finally able to connect to someone after being closed off for so long.

Now she lay curled against me, her breathing deep and peaceful. I traced the curve of her shoulder, memorising the warm softness of her skin. How had I let myself fall so deep? Every instinct screamed at me to run, to protect her from what I was. But the wolf was fully imprinted now, and the man ... God help me, the man was just as lost.

The first wave hit without warning.

A tingling brightness that made my blood leap in my veins. Maeve's heartbeat drummed suddenly loud, her sweet scent waking the beast.

No. Not here. Not with her so close.

I rolled from the bed, my feet silent on the floorboards, my senses suddenly acute, spots dancing in my vision as I fought what was coming.

"Fen?" She stirred, reaching for me. "What's wrong?"

I stumbled from the room, barely making it to the door. The change was coming fast. The wolf could sense its mate nearby, the full moon stripping away what little control I had left.

"Go back to sleep," I managed through gritted teeth. "I just need some air."

She sat up, the sheet falling away. "Let me come with you—"

"No—" The word came out a half-growl. "Please. Just ... stay here."

I fled into the night, my skin already burning, my bones tingling and morphing as the change took hold. I stripped, flinging my clothes into a dark hollow, and reached the tree line at the edge of the reserve just as the strength drained from my limbs. I collapsed forward with a grunt, the dark magic taking hold, large paws hitting the dirt, ears pricked to the chaos of night noises, the breeze ruffling my fur. I started bounding away into the shadows ... then froze.

Maeve's scent called me back to the cottage—vanilla and jasmine and a warm musky sweetness that was all her. My wolf wanted to wheel around and return to her, be near and protect as instinct said I must—but that part of me was too volatile. Too unpredictable. Why had I let myself believe I deserved her love?

I was too dangerous. Too broken. Too cursed.

I would ruin her. Destroy everything she believed in, everything she held dear. And I loved her too much to risk it. Yet still I stood there, at the edge of the trees, half-concealed by moon shadows, watching as her silhouette appeared in the window.

A growl rumbled through me.

She is mine and I am hers ... nothing else should matter. So why did I quake with the terror of losing her? Or worse, that she would discover what I'd done and hate me as much as I hated myself?

The moon mocked me with its huge silver eye as I slunk along the edge of the forest, torn between the need to protect her ... and my impossible, fated addiction to her love.

26

———————

MAEVE

THE NIGHT AIR was crisp against my bare arms as I followed the garden path into the darkness. Something felt off—Fen's shaking had jolted me awake, his uneven breathing setting off my internal alarms. Now he'd vanished completely.

"Fen?" My voice barely broke through the shadows among the trees. "Where are you?"

The moon drifted overhead, its light silvering the edges of my plants and shrubs, lighting up my little greenhouse and shining off the cottage roof. What had Fen said all those weeks ago? *When it's full, we change. Become something lost and broken. Shunned by the world.*

What had he meant? He'd almost made the moon sound alive, as though it controlled him. As though it had power over him. I stared up at it, trying to picture it coming to life, wreaking havoc on the Harkness family—but all I saw was a polished silver button stitched onto the dark fabric of the night.

"Always so mysterious," I murmured. "Why won't you just tell me the truth? It can't be all that shocking." After all, two years ago I had watched my husband get mauled to death by a wolf—how could anything be worse than that?

A flicker caught my eye in the murky twilight. I walked towards it. "Fen?"

The silhouette of a wolf emerged from the shadows. Its sleek grey fur melded with the surrounding gloom, and its eyes glinted like twin orbs of silver as it watched me intently.

"Oh. It's you." Fen had cautioned me about approaching it, but it seemed more curious than threatening. Besides, it had rescued me in the forest, I was hardly going to chase it away. Not if it was hungry and prowling for food. "There's some nice tasty bacon in the fridge."

The wolf's ears flicked forward at my voice.

"Sounds good, huh?"

It whined, its pale eyes mirroring the moonlight. My mysterious protector. But something was different tonight. Instead of its usual calm presence, the wolf seemed agitated, shifting from paw to paw.

I reached out slowly. "It's okay. I won't hurt you." But as I eased forward, the moonlight flared off my silver ring, and the wolf yelped, shying away from it. Lips curled, teeth bared, it let out a low snarl. The warning was soft, but it was unmistakable. *Don't come any closer.* Then it turned and fled, leaving me alone in the moonlight.

I waited up all night, but Fen never came back. When dawn finally broke, I was still sitting on my back steps, turning my wolf ring around and around on my finger, my brain in overdrive. Where was he? And why had he left in such a rush, not even taking the time to tell me?

Tomorrow, he'd skirt around my questions as he always did, and I would let him. Because the last thing I wanted was to drive him away. Alec had hated my nagging, even though I was only trying to save him from the drink. The Lambs had their own family curse, only it wasn't the moon controlling them but booze.

Fen was different. Aside from his secrecy at certain times of the month, we spent the rest of our time making everyone else sick with how in love we were. Kitty was always shaking her head in mock horror. *Get a room, losers.* Liam was more reserved, although Fen said he was genuinely happy for us. Nan, on the other hand, was full of her usual warnings. *He's a Harkness, Maeve. Whatever you do, please be careful.*

So what was this one thorn in our happiness? What was Fen hiding from me? And more importantly—was I ready to know the truth?

27

MAEVE

Morning sunlight streamed through my bedroom window, warming the sheets tangled around us. Fen slept deeply beside me, one arm draped possessively across my waist. In sleep, the tension melted from his face, making him look younger. Vulnerable.

But as I traced the line of his jaw, last night's strangeness crept back. The way he'd trembled before fleeing into the darkness. The wolf's warning snarl. The long hours I'd waited, until he'd finally slipped back into bed just before dawn.

"You're thinking too loud." His voice was rough with sleep as his eyes fluttered open.

"Where did you go last night?"

"Couldn't sleep." He nuzzled into my neck, trying to distract me. "Went for a walk."

"All night?"

"Mm." His lips found that sensitive spot below my ear and nibbled there. "Needed to clear my head."

I pulled back slightly, studying his face. "Fen, what's going on?"

"Nothing." But he wouldn't quite meet my eyes. "Everything's fine."

Everything wasn't fine. Nan's warning echoed for the millionth time in my head. *Fen's sister believed in that curse with all her heart. How do we know it didn't pass from one family member to another? That it won't somehow pass onto you?*

Was that what haunted Fen? Did he truly believe he was cursed, doomed never to love? The idea seemed ridiculous in the warm morning light. But then I remembered the way he'd communed with the black wolf, how he never seemed afraid of the creatures that everyone else in town fled from in fear.

And the grey wolf—my mysterious protector who appeared whenever I needed help, who seemed to know me...

What was it about Fen and those damn wolves?

He had them everywhere.

Inscribed on the mysterious athame he kept near the bird cages. The framed illustrations in his study of a wolf pack hunting in the woods. His tattoos that I'd mapped a hundred times with my fingers and tongue. Even the beautiful ring he had paid an artist in town to craft especially for me, with its eternally fleeing wolf-mates.

For heaven's sake, he and Liam even rescued wolves that the rest of Riverwood shunned—

I gasped, sitting bolt upright in the bed. *When the moon's full, we become something lost and broken, shunned by the world.*

"Mae?" Fen sat up beside me, brushing my cheek with his thumb. "You okay?"

"Fine," I said too quickly.

He kissed my forehead and slipped from the bed, gathering his clothes.

"I should get to the clinic. Liam's got some dingo pups coming in. Their mum was another one of Derek's casualties."

Normally I'd have had a few choice words for my scumbag brother-in-law, but this time I let it go.

"See you tonight?" I asked in a flat voice, already knowing Fen's answer.

He paused at the door, glancing through the window. "I'm keeping the pups at my place, so I'll need to settle them in for a few days. I'll call you next week?"

"Hmm." Whatever.

"Sure you're okay, Maeve? I can hang around if you need me to?"

I shook my head, not trusting myself to speak. And when he strode back and cupped his hands around my face, kissing me so tenderly it all but broke my heart, I almost crumbled.

Almost.

"Love you, Mae," he whispered, giving my hair a gentle tug. On any other day, I'd have melted to hear him say it. But I couldn't even unclamp my teeth long enough to say it back. Instead, I let him walk away, my silence yawning between us like a black hole.

And then he was gone.

Riding off into the sunrise while I was now the one running late. My thoughts spinning too wildly for me to budge.

Tonight, I'd visit him.

Take him by surprise and find out what he was really up to. I knew it wasn't another woman because not once in the past few months had I ever questioned his devotion.

I just needed to know what the heck was *really* going on with him.

Because curses weren't real.

They couldn't be.

Could they?

I touched my wolf ring, remembering the night I first met him on the forest road. He'd never spoken about what happened to him that night. Who beat him up. Shot him. And I had given up asking.

Only now, some crazy thoughts were creeping in. The way his eyes had shone silver in the moonlight that night. The way his injuries—the bullet wound on his hip, his mangled wrist, his bruised ribs—had mirrored those of the wolf I'd just rescued from Derek.

"Not to mention how quickly they healed."

Fen's words drifted back, and I shivered. *Riverwood has some pretty shady things going on. Not everyone here is what they seem.*

"Including you, Fen Harkness."

Maybe it was time to stop pretending everything was normal. Maybe it was time to face whatever Fen was hiding—no matter how impossible it seemed.

After all, I'd learned the hard way with Alec that secrets could destroy you. I wouldn't let that happen with Fen. Not when I was already in too deep.

28

THE WOLF

I BOUNDED UNDER THE MOON, my paws silent on the damp earth as I raced the river along its edge, the night darkening around me. So many trails to follow. Rabbit. Possum. Little squeakers. But larger prey, too. Wild piglet and goat, a lone deer—

Far away, near home, a light bloomed in the sky. The faint rumble of a car motor echoed through the forest. I pricked my ears, nose twitching as I stopped to taste the air. But it was my heart that sensed her first.

Maeve.

Far away still, but out here in the forest instead of safe in town. Had she come to find me? Had something happened with Derek again, had he hurt her?

I changed direction and sped away from the river, back towards home. My body trembling at what I might find, knowing only my need to see that she was all right.

The moon rode high, its silver light burning in my blood, giving me speed as I neared the house. It lay in darkness, the surrounding bushland quiet. Another scent drifted somewhere near—motor oil and musky sweat—but the approaching car interested me more.

Headlights swept the driveway, and I melted into the shadows of the twisted old gum trees beside the house.

"Fen?" Maeve's voice carried on the night air as she climbed out of her car and walked along the path to the front steps. "Are you home?"

My ears twitched at her voice. She banged on the door, then hurried along the gravel towards the rear of the house. I followed silently.

"The lights are on, your bike's here..." She paused, her blood pounding so loudly through her warm body that I felt it in my chest. "Fen?"

I stalked out of the shadows, circling behind her, as I had at the cottage weeks ago, growling softly.

She spun around, her breath catching. "Oh!"

I advanced on her, herding her past the trunk of the old red gum towards where she'd parked in the driveway. Another growl rumbled from me, warning her to leave. To run.

But she didn't.

She stood her ground, her chin lifting as she studied me. "It's you," she whispered. "My wild wolf. I'm not scared of you, so you can stop growling at me. I'm not here to hurt you."

I bared my teeth, flattening my ears to show her I wasn't a tame creature to be played with but a dangerous predator who could take her down in an eyeblink.

You won't. She knows that. You would die to protect her, and she knows that, too.

She stepped closer. "Please don't run away again. You can trust me, I promise."

As she eased nearer, reaching out a trembling hand, her scent hit me—the warm, musky sweetness catching me off guard. I froze as her hand brushed my muzzle, the silver ring on her finger making bright contact with my nose—

I yelped and sprang away.

Too late. The shudder started deep in my bones and rippled through my body, my fur electrified as the curse's dark magic crackled across my skin, retreating. The smells and sounds around me dimmed, waves of panic washing over me, the darkness throbbing as the wolf in me lunged forward, wanting to protect my female...

And the man collapsed into her arms.

29

MAEVE

HIS SOLID WEIGHT almost threw me off balance, his skin fever-hot and slick with sweat where moments ago there was fur. I staggered back, trying to keep us both upright as I held him, trying to process what I'd just seen—one moment the grey wolf was there, the next Fen was falling naked into my arms.

His face pressed against my neck, his ragged breathing hot against my skin. His hold on me tightened.

"Maeve, I'm sorry."

A rush of heat surged through my veins, followed by a chill. Was I dreaming? I felt so awake, so alive, but this had to be a dream, right? How could this be real? *It's the curse*, my mind whispered, and deep down, I knew it was true. Even as my mind struggled, I could feel the truth of it in my bones.

"Why didn't you tell me?" I whispered, still hugging him tightly.

Fen looked up, his eyes meeting mine—the same eyes I had seen in the wolf's face, pale silvery green.

"I tried to tell you," he said, his voice rough. He straightened but kept his hands at my waist, as though afraid I might bolt. "But I couldn't risk losing you."

"I'm still here." I touched his cheek, wiping away a smudge of dirt. "Talking to a guy who was just a wolf. I'd say I'm handling it pretty well, all things considered."

He frowned. "You suspected."

"Not exactly *this*. But yeah, something wasn't adding up." I scraped my fingernails gently over the stubble on his jaw, searching his pale eyes. "Please, Fen. No more secrets between us. I want to know everything—about the curse, your family. Your ... wolf. Even if it's completely crazy."

"I will, Maeve. I promise." The tension in his shoulders eased. "Just let me grab some clothes. I'm feeling kinda vulnerable right now. And not just because I'm naked."

While he dressed, I paced up and down the verandah in front of the empty owl cage. Was I dreaming? No, of course not. But I felt as if my world had shifted off its axis and was now spinning out of control towards some new reality.

The grey wolf—my wolf—was Fen? A shiver ran up my spine. I kept searching for flaws in the logic, hoping to uncover a lie, but everything just seemed to fit together all the more perfectly. The wolf protecting me from Derek. His forays near my home. The wild dog I almost hit with my car, and then Fen by the roadside naked, just as he'd been tonight—

"I can see your cogs spinning." Fen was fully dressed in jeans and a flannel shirt. He steered me down the steps into the garden, shoving a chocolate bar into my hand. "It'll help with the shock."

The chocolate was gone before we'd walked ten paces, and he was right. I felt better.

"Where are we going?"

"I'm gonna tell you everything, Maeve. The whole tangled

history, like I promised. But before anything else, I'd like you to meet a couple of people."

We followed the gravel path past the veggie patch, around the gnarled apple trees heavy with fruit. The verandah light shone softly behind us, moths swirling, the bright glow casting patterns around us as we walked.

We stopped at the far edge of the garden where two simple gravestones stood beneath a massive pine tree. No dates, just their names carved into the weathered granite.

"My parents," Fen said quietly. "Evelina and Emeric Harkness."

I waited, barely breathing. For months I'd been longing to know about Fen's past, but now that he was on the brink of telling me—after what I'd just seen—my stomach started to churn. Getting close to him, opening up and trusting him had been surprisingly easy, especially after ten years of guarding my heart around Alec. But Fen was full of secrets, and they seemed way darker and more dangerous than I felt ready to handle.

Fen trailed his fingertips across the pitted stone of his father's grave. "Our family has carried this burden for generations," he finally said, looking over at me.

"The curse?" I asked softly.

He nodded, his eyes distant. "My ancestors brought it with them from Europe. The Harknesses have always been ... different. But we managed to build a life here, away from those who hunted us in the past."

"And the Lambs?"

"The Lambs were hunters there, too. They followed us here."

"That's what Betty meant when she said the Lambs avoided your family. She said you were dangerous."

"I am. But then so is Betty Lamb. She's more than she appears, Maeve."

"I never much liked her. So controlling. And the way she used to look at me, like she wanted to—" I rubbed my arms. "Exterminate me like an insect."

"Betty sees people as pawns in her game." Fen's voice hardened. "My mother was Evelina Snow before she married. From the richest family in Riverwood. Betty wanted her to marry into the Lamb family—to strengthen their position here. But Mum, bless her, fell for my dad instead."

"If he was anything like you, I can't blame her."

A ghost of a smile touched his lips. "Dad was an agronomist, and when he came here to Australia he fell in love with the wilderness. He took up market gardening, and became an avid conservationist. Gentle, brilliant with animals, too. Mum used to say it was love at first sight. For them both."

Gum leaves dropped around us, spiraling gently in the night air. Fen caught one and crushed it between his fingers.

"Betty never forgave them. She'd spent her life studying our kind, learning our weaknesses."

"Wait." I pictured Alec's grandmother with her elegant suits and cold eyes. "Betty knows about the curse?"

"The Lambs have always known. It's what they do—hunt our kind. Have for centuries." Fen's jaw tightened. "My parents thought they were safe here. Dad was researching the curse, looking for ways to manage it. Control it."

"And the Lambs found out?"

Fen nodded, digging his hands deep into his pockets, hunching against an invisible threat as he looked over. "That's why I keep people at arm's length, Maeve. I'm friendly enough in town, but never too close. It's too easy to slip up, so it seemed safer just to keep to myself."

I went closer to the graves, my shadow falling over them. "The curse can't be broken?"

Fen frowned up at the sky, his face carved by the pale moonlight. "Dad discovered something. He inherited the athame—passed down through our family for generations—and learned that it has the power to transfer the curse."

"Transfer?"

He nodded. "Three drops of blood and a whispered spell will shift it from one person to another. But it's dangerous. And there's a catch."

"A catch?"

"The person freed from the curse forgets they ever knew the person who took it."

"Bloody hell."

"Yeah."

"Fen, what happened to your parents?"

His voice grew hollow. "Dad was getting close to something. He and Mum worked together—she was an astronomer at the observatory, and began studying the effects of moon cycles on the curse. They discovered patterns in Betty's activities, records going back further than should have been possible."

"You mean Betty's older than she lets on?"

He nodded, tensing his shoulders against the night. "Betty somehow found out what they knew. It was the night of a blood moon. A lunar eclipse. The four of us shifted and went on the hunt. Mum and Dad always took us into the deep woods, far from town. They thought it was safer for us kids. Only that night, Betty's brothers were waiting. With silver bullets."

"Silver actually hurts you?"

"It can kill us. Nothing else is permanent." He drew a shaky breath. "They shot my father first. Mum and I saw them bring him down. She looked at me and gave a shrill bark, her hackles bristling. I knew what she was saying. Run, Fen. Run back to the den and be safe. So I started running to one of our safe places in the forest. But when I looked behind, she'd gone back to him. She launched herself at the men, but ... they killed her too. Right in front of me."

I went over and covered his trembling hands with my own, feeling the warmth of his skin, the life in him that had survived despite everything.

"You were just a kid, Fen. You couldn't have saved them. The hunters would have killed you, too."

"That's what Erin used to say. It never stopped me blaming myself, though."

I remembered what Nan had said about Fen's sister going off the rails.

"Why did Erin run away?"

"That night in the woods, she was on a fox's trail and didn't see what happened. But later, she smelled their blood. She's the one who found them." His voice cracked, his fingers tightening around mine. "When shifters die, they revert to human form. She found them near each other, their bodies riddled with silver bullets. She understood what it meant—someone knew what we were."

"Dear God."

"The hunters never found the athame," Fen continued after a moment. "Dad kept it a secret, even from Betty."

"And Derek? Does he know what you are?"

"He suspects, but he doesn't understand the full history. Maybe Betty has mellowed with age, because the Lambs never hunt with silver now. Just regular bullets that only slow us down."

"Like that night I found you on the forest road?"

Fen's eyes met mine, his gaze wary, as if waiting for me to freak out. "You're taking this surprisingly well, Maeve."

"Maybe I've been waiting my whole life to believe in something impossible." The night breeze picked up, bringing the smell of rain, sending tiny shivers over my skin. "Or maybe I just love you enough to accept all of you. Even the parts with fur and fangs."

Fen's breath caught. He leaned forward, taking my face in his palms and resting his forehead against mine.

"Maeve," he whispered, so quietly I strained to hear. "After what happened to Alec, I'll understand if you never want to see me again. But just know this. My heart is yours now. Until the day it stops beating, and beyond, it's yours. That's how it is with wolves. With me. Always, okay?"

30

MAEVE

"I FEEL A BIT LIGHTHEADED," I admitted as we walked back to the house. "All this talk about the curse. I'm trying to take it in, but it's a lot."

Fen pulled another chocolate bar from his pocket, a little soft after contact with his body heat.

"Eat."

"You're my hero." I peeled it open and scarfed it down, the sugar hit reviving me. I balled the wrapper and slid it into my jeans pocket with the other one, and as I did, my silver ring glinted in the moonlight.

I looked at Fen. "If silver can hurt you, then why did you give me the ring?"

"To protect you. From me. Touching it won't hurt me, only weaken the curse. You'd need a bullet or a knife to do serious damage."

"So that's why you shifted when I touched you before—the curse faded because of the ring. Is that why you're not shifting back?"

He watched me in the moonlight, then nodded. "Are you scared of me now, Maeve? Now that you know what I am?"

I thought back to the night Alec died, the flickering campfire light and the terrifying shadow that sprang from the darkness.

"I should be. Though to be honest, I'm more scared *for* you. After what you told me about the Lambs, and your parents. But Fen—" His name caught in my throat as I searched his face in the semi-dark. "I feel a little sick that I had to find out by accident. Don't you trust me?"

His eyes gleamed in the moonlight, shadows swarming over his face as he took my hand. "Come on."

We returned to the house and climbed the verandah steps. Fen moved to the wall where his antique tool collection hung. "I trust you now," he said quietly, lifting down the athame, its silver blade catching the moonlight. He handled it carefully by the wooden hilt. "That's why I'm giving you this. It's the one thing that can stop my wolf. Permanently."

My heart clenched. "I don't want to stop it, Fen. Not if it means losing you."

"Keep it, okay? So you never doubt my trust again." His breath caught as he gently gripped the silver blade, pushing the wooden hilt into my palm.

"No, Fen. I don't need—"

My skin tingled where it touched the ancient knife, the smooth wood strangely icy, as though something old and dead lived inside it. A dark energy crackled into my fingers and up my arm, circling my heart like a swarm of bees. Images began exploding in my mind. *I'm in the forest with Alec, it's dark except for the campfire's flickering flames—*

"Maeve?" Strong fingers gripped my arms, steadying me. I sagged against him, wanting to drop the knife, but my fingers were clenched like stone around the wooden hilt, its toxic magic humming through me, reeling me back into the past, to the night everything crumbled—

The campfire burns low, making shadows flicker through the trees. Alec sways on his feet, whiskey bottle dangling from his fingers.

"You're a chore to be with, Maeve." His words slur together. "Always scared. Always careful. When will you learn to live a little, eh?"

"I brought us out here, didn't I?"

He grips the bottle tightly. "If you think camping in this dreary shit-hole is going to change anything between us, you're dead wrong."

"Please." I back away. "You're drunk. Let's just go to sleep—"

The bottle shatters against a tree near my head. His fist follows, catching my cheekbone. I stumble and fall. His boot connects with my ribs, again and again, until dots dance in my eyes, and a single thought revolves like a curse in my brain. I wish he was dead, I wish with all my heart I was free of him...

Then I see it—a massive grey shape launching from the shadows. Its shaggy fur, the sharp ears flattened back, the silver gleam in its wild eyes...

Alec's scream cuts off in a wet gurgle as the wolf's powerful jaws close around his throat, its snowy white muzzle turning crimson in the dying firelight—

The memory released me and I staggered back, trembling so hard I could barely stand. Blinking at Fen in horror.

The grey wolf. My protector.

The one who'd been watching over me all this time.

Fen.

I stared as if seeing him for the first time. Seeing the monster he truly was.

"You killed him." The words felt like shards in my mouth, knives in my heart. "You killed Alec."

He didn't deny it. Just stood there, shoulders bowed under the weight of his secret. But his eyes. God, the pain in his eyes as he stared back at me—like watching someone drown from shore. I couldn't bear to look any longer. With a shaky breath, I turned away, pounding down the steps and into the yard.

My wolf. Fen.

He killed Alec.

And all this time he knew, while I had been falling in love with the thing I feared most. Every touch, every kiss, every moment of trust was built on a lie. Nan had been right, after all. I'd let down my guard and now the monster had come out to crush my dreams of a happy ending.

"Maeve, please." His boots thumped down the steps as he came after me. "Let me explain."

At the sound of his voice so near, right behind me, how ragged it sounded, how broken—something inside me shattered. The careful walls I'd built around my heart, the hope I'd finally allowed myself to feel. Piece by piece they crumbled, fell away. In their place, the blaze of something harsh and cruel ignited in my chest. I wanted to lash out and hurt him as he'd hurt me.

As he'd hurt Alec.

I gripped the athame tightly and turned around, rushing at Fen and pressing the sharp blade against his throat.

"All these months, you've been lying to me. Not only about what you are—but about what you did. To Alec. Did you ever think it was something I might need to know? Before we—" I swallowed a sob, stepping closer till my body was almost against his, the athame's edge sliding dangerously against his throat.

"Drop the knife, Maeve," he whispered, his nostrils flaring. "You're upset, and I get it. We need to talk. But right now you're messing with something with the power to destroy us both."

"Actually, the thought of destroying something feels pretty damn tempting."

"Maeve." His voice broke on my name, and a tremor went through him. The colour drained from his face, his eyes flaring dull silver. "Come back to the house, we'll talk it through. And for God's sake, drop the knife. I can't protect you if you weaken the curse."

"You can't hurt me either."

"I would never hurt you."

I stood rigid, not moving, keeping the blade steady against the pulsing skin beneath his jaw. Tears streaked my cheeks as my world crashed around me. The forest that had started to feel like home now pressed in, dark and suffocating. Everything I thought I knew about love, about trust, about my strength—all of it dying inside me with no hope of salvation.

And the worst part? Some wild, treacherous part of me understood that he'd killed Alec to protect me. He had answered my silent prayer that night, freeing me from Alec, delivering me from my tormentor. And that same part whispered that maybe, just maybe, I would have done the same for him.

And that terrified me most of all.

31

FEN

I COULD SMELL THE BLOOD. The tiny, hot droplet beading on my throat where the silver blade had nicked the skin. Rich and metallic in the night, a reminder of the athame's power over me, its cold blade calling to the darkness inside me. If she cut just a fraction deeper into the skin, drew a trickle more, then the curse would start to leave me. And when it did, I would forget her. Forget that I loved her, that she had loved me.

Dying I could deal with.

But forgetting her?

"Maeve, drop the knife now. Or use it on me if you want to. Just be quick because I can't stand the thought of losing you."

Her hand began to tremble. She was more beautiful than I'd ever seen her—eyes wild and fierce, her hair escaping in coils around her shoulders. Her careful mask stripped away.

"If I cut you," she said, her voice almost a growl. "If I draw your blood—will it break the curse?"

I didn't try to move, didn't try to defend myself. There was no defence for what I'd done—her pain was my doing, maybe I deserved to lose her. One last lie, and I would tell it to save her, despite what I'd promised.

"No," I ground out. "Nothing will break it."

A sound tore from her throat—half laugh, half sob. "Then I don't want the stupid knife!" She raised her arm and threw the athame at the trees, the blade glittering in the moonlight as it arced into the night and disappeared. She pushed me away. "And I don't want you either!"

She turned and ran, and I let her go. The wolf inside me howled to follow, to explain, to make her understand. But I'd done enough damage. Maybe this was better—a clean break before I could hurt her anymore. Before the curse could claim her too.

Her car engine roared to life, headlights cutting through the darkness. But as she pulled away, another set of lights blinked on along the shadowy verge. A white ute lurched onto the road behind her, engine gunning.

Derek.

The wolf exploded from me before I could think, my blood still thin and cold after the athame's touch. It should have stopped me, slowed me, but even in my weakened state the part of me that needed to protect her was stronger.

My paws hit the dirt running, my powerful legs eating up the distance as I bounded out onto the road. Derek's ute vanished ahead of me and quickly disappeared.

I howled into the night. What was Derek planning? He'd been waiting. Watching. And now he had Maeve exactly where he wanted her—alone and vulnerable.

Trees blurred past as I raced after them, my heart thundering with more than exertion. I had tried so hard to protect her, to keep her safe from my dangerous world. But now I'd driven her straight into Derek's trap.

If anything happens to her...

A snarl rumbled in my chest as I pushed faster, harder, my teeth bared. I'd killed once to protect her.

I'd do it again without hesitation.

32

MAEVE

Tears blurred the road ahead as I pressed the accelerator harder. Everything inside me felt raw, bleeding. Fen had killed Alec. He had watched over me for months, letting me fall in love with him while keeping his deadly secret. Now it was over, the trust we'd built so carefully hanging between us like a fragile, broken thread.

Headlights flashed in my rearview mirror. A white car emerged through the dust cloud behind me, then pulled out to overtake. But instead of zooming ahead, it swerved beside me, forcing me onto the verge.

"What the—" I gripped the wheel and drove my foot down hard on the brakes, but that only sent me into a spin. My wheels skidded on the loose gravel, the Lancer careening out of control, the roadside trees looming. The world tilted and whirled until everything crashed to a stop.

Before I could catch my breath, my door wrenched open. Rough hands dragged me out into the night.

"Hey, little wildcat." Derek's breath was hot against my

face, reeking of whiskey and cigarette smoke. "We're gonna have ourselves a party."

"Let me go!" I thrashed against him, but he only laughed, dragging me away from the car and deeper into the trees. The rifle slung over his shoulder clattered against me as we struggled, the strap digging into his beefy chest.

"Can't control you, can I?" His fingers dug into my arms. "My brother couldn't tame you. And when I tried, you ran straight to that monster instead."

"Derek, please—"

"Saw the whole thing back there. Heard everything. How that beast killed my brother. And you..." His voice cracked. "You love him. You couldn't love Alec, couldn't love me, but you love that animal."

As I struggled harder, he swung up his arm and slammed his elbow into the side of my head. My teeth clacked together and the night greyed around me. I felt myself slipping, but I fought it, just as I'd learned to do with Alec. I jerked my knee into him, but he dodged sideways and hit me again, the sharp sting of blood throbbing on my lip.

Something glinted in his hand—the athame. My heart stopped. He must have been watching, like he said. Seen where it fell. He raised it to my throat, pricking the delicate flesh under my chin.

"Stop wriggling, damn you. You're just making it worse for yourself."

I kicked him in the shin, but he only grunted, dragging me further along the wide dirt trail, stumbling over tyre tracks carved deep in the ground. When we reached the edge of an old clearcut area, saplings pushing through the thin soil between the stumps, he stopped.

"Been waiting for this." His eyes gleamed, his face glistening with sweat. "I've been tracking that big grey bastard for months. And now I know exactly what he is." His grin was savage in the moonlight. "He dies tonight."

"No—"

"Oh yes." He jerked me closer, his eyes fever-bright. "And you're going to help me kill him. Because we both know he'll come for you. He always does."

Icy fear washed over me. Derek had planned this perfectly—using me as bait, knowing Fen would come. And now he had the one weapon that could destroy him.

A howl split the night, somewhere close.

Derek's grin widened. "Right on time."

33

MAEVE

"FEN, NO!" The cry tore from my throat as a massive grey shape launched from the darkness. "It's a trap!"

But the wolf was already airborne, powerful jaws snapping, eyes ablaze. Derek shoved me aside. As the wolf drove him to the ground, he rolled sideways, the athame flashing silver in the moonlight as he thrust it into the wolf's chest. There was a terrible yelp as the blade sank deep into the animal's side, near his heart.

The wolf thrashed, trying to twist free of the knife. Blood matted his fur black in the gloomy half-light. His pale eyes found mine, filled with pain and something else—his fierce need to protect me, even now. He barked at me, once, his lips drawn back and hackles bristling along his spine. I knew what he was saying. *Run, Maeve. Run back to the den and be safe—*

My heart cracked open. All my confusion, my anger at his lies, fell away. He would have known this was a trap, caught a whiff of Derek's sweat and felt the athame's presence. But he'd leaped right into it, anyway.

For me.

Knowing what Derek was planning. Knowing he wouldn't survive.

I lunged forward, wrapping my hands around the athame's hilt. The blade burned cold against my palms, but this time my mind stayed clear as I wrenched it free. The wolf stumbled, a whine escaping him.

Derek reached for his rifle. "You won't get far, Maeve. Either of you."

I slashed the athame toward him, forcing him back. "Stay away from us!"

He laughed, all the meanness in his heart bubbling up into the half-crazed sound. "Us? You're choosing that monster? After what he did?"

"The only monster here is you."

The wolf struggled to his feet beside me, swaying. Blood dripped steadily from his wound. We had to get out of here and find help. We couldn't return to Fen's house, that was the first place Derek would look for us. But there must be somewhere. The den. I had no idea where to find it. But Fen would.

Derek raised his rifle, sighting down the barrel. "I'll kill you both if I have to."

I grabbed a handful of the wolf's fur, and we broke for the trees together. The first shot cracked past my ear as we plunged into the darkness. The second splintered bark beside my head.

"Run!" I screamed, though I didn't know if I was yelling at Fen or myself.

We crashed through the undergrowth, away from the clearcut area into the deeper woods, more shots echoing behind us. The wolf's breath came in ragged pants, his powerful body trembling. But he matched his pace to mine, staying between me and danger even as his life bled out of him and soaked into the forest floor.

Everything I thought I knew about love and monsters and

happy ever afters shifted in that moment. Because here was the truth—the monster I'd feared for so long was no danger to me —rather, he'd been protecting me from the real monsters all along. And now it was my turn to protect him.

34

MAEVE

WE STUMBLED THROUGH THE DARKNESS, the wolf's massive body growing heavier against me with each step. Blood streamed from the wound near his heart, leaving a trail I prayed Derek wouldn't find. But it wasn't just the blood loss—something darker was happening. The athame's magic seemed to be draining Fen's spirit, dimming the silvery light in his eyes.

"Stay with me," I whispered, half-dragging him forward. "Please, Fen."

His breath came in ragged pants, but his eyes stayed on me —until a branch cracked somewhere behind us—Derek was getting closer. The wolf's ears swivelled back at the sound and he tried to turn and face the threat, but his once-powerful legs buckled under him.

A shadow detached itself from the trees ahead. Another wolf, black as night, bounded toward us. Before I could cry out, it shifted in a blur of motion, fur melting away until a man stood before us—tall, dark-haired, his skin a map of tattoos.

"Liam!"

He moved to support Fen's other side. "The den. Quickly."

Together we hauled Fen's body downhill a way, then through a narrow opening between boulders. Cool darkness enveloped us as we entered the den, moonlight filtering through a gap in the rocks above us, picking out tiny ferns and damp crevices. The wolf's claws scrabbled weakly against bare ground as we laid him down.

I collapsed beside him, cradling his massive head in my lap. His pale eyes found me in the gloom, and I saw the recognition there, the love.

"Liam, help him," I pleaded, not taking my eyes from Fen's. My silver ring caught the moonlight as I ran trembling fingers through his fur. "Please."

Liam knelt beside his friend, feeling around the jagged edges of the wound with gentle fingers. Blood seeped steadily from the gash, darkening Fen's once-bright fur and forming tiny streams that trickled onto the dirt below. Its metallic scent made the air feel heavy and unbreathable as panic clawed inside me.

"Why isn't he changing," I almost shouted, clutching Fen tighter. "My ring forced him to shift before, but nothing's happening. Why isn't it working?"

Fen whimpered softly, pressing his muzzle against my hand as if trying to comfort me.

"The wound is deep," Liam said, his voice tight. "It'll take time, but he'll—"

His words cut off as a drunken bellow came from somewhere outside, followed by the crack of rifle fire.

I flinched, but Fen's eyes never left mine, and the love I saw there tore my heart. I remembered the athame, suddenly aware of its weight in my back pocket.

I pulled it out, hands shaking. "Can we use this somehow? To reverse it?"

Liam's nostrils flared as he inhaled. "Derek used this on him?"

I could smell the blood on it, too. Fen's blood. "Yes."

A muscle tightened in Liam's jaw. "Then we're too late, Maeve. It's already over."

I wanted to argue, but Fen's words came back. *The athame is the one thing that can stop my wolf.* The panic I'd been fighting crashed through me, a tidal wave of icy blackness that stole my breath and buckled me over the big dog, gasping. I dropped the cursed athame onto the ground beside me, wishing I'd never laid eyes on it.

Another shot rang out, closer this time, and Fen tried to lift his head, a low growl vibrating through his chest.

"Stay still," I whispered, smoothing my fingers over his fur. "Save your strength."

But there was no strength left to save. I could feel it now—the curse retreating like a dark tide, sweeping away the future I'd dreamed for us. The talks we'd never have. The nights under stars. The mornings waking in his arms, feeling loved and at peace.

"Fen?" I gripped his shaggy scruff and pressed my forehead to his. "What can I do? How can I fix this?"

Liam reached over and gripped my shoulder. "You can't fix it. Not this time."

"But I stitched him before," I insisted, tears streaming down my face. "And he healed quickly, he—"

"He's dying, Maeve."

"No," I whispered, my voice breaking. "He'll get better, like before."

"The curse is leaving him." Liam ran a tattooed hand along the big creature's shaggy back. "He doesn't have long."

The wolf's breathing grew shallower, his massive chest barely rising now. But his eyes—his beautiful, knowing eyes—remained fixed on mine.

"No." I buried my fingers in his fur, feeling how solid, how still he suddenly seemed, as though the weight of the darkness had entered him and was dragging him under. "Please don't leave me, Fen. There has to be something—"

Gunfire cracked the stillness outside. Derek was getting closer. How much longer before he found us? Before it was all over?

Liam rose, moving toward the entrance, the shadows already bending and blurring around him. "I'll hold him off as long as I can."

I barely noticed him leave. All I could see was Fen's life bleeding away, taking a part of me with it. The best part. The bravest part.

His breath came in shallow gasps now, each one a battle. I pressed my lips to his nose, and his body shuddered against me. I held on tighter, as if I could anchor him to this world through sheer force of will.

"I love you," I whispered fiercely. "Do you hear me? I love you, and I'm not giving you up without a fight."

His eyes met mine, and in them I saw not just the wolf, but the man—my Fen, my heart—looking back at me through the veil between this world and forever.

"I should have told you sooner," I whispered against his fur, my tears mingling with his blood. "I wasted so much time being afraid. But I'm not any more. I love you, Fen. Wolf and all."

Love was a curse, Nan claimed—and after ten years of marriage to Alec, I had come to believe it, too. Never straying from the path, never taking a risk. Well, not anymore. Love was all I had left now. The one thing in my life that was truly worth living for.

Worth dying for.

35

MAEVE

THE WOLF LAY STILL in my arms, his massive body growing heavier as his breathing grew shallower, more laboured. Blood matted his grey fur around the wound, turning it black in the dim light of the den.

Gunfire cracked outside, but it was far away now. Liam had lured Derek southwards, back towards town, but my brother-in-law wouldn't give up that easily. Now that he knew what Fen was, and what he meant to me, Derek would track us relentlessly. He wouldn't give up until we were both dead.

My tears rained onto the wolf's snowy muzzle, leaving little dents in the fur. I needed a weapon. So that when Derek came for us, I'd be ready. The athame lay beside me where I'd dropped it, its silver blade still stained with Fen's blood.

I picked it up. It barely tingled now against my bloodstained palm. No more memories exploded from it, no more dark energy crackling through me. Just the faint echo of Fen's voice as we stood beside his parents' graves.

It has the power to transfer the curse.

I sat up suddenly, trying to recall what else he'd said. "Something about blood," I whispered. "Three drops. And a spell—"

The wolf blinked, and a faint growl rumbled up out of his chest. He struggled to sit up, but I placed my hand on his back and soothed him down again.

"The answer's been here all along," I told him, tracing my fingers over the script etched into the athame's blade, an ancient language I couldn't read. But when I flipped the knife over, there was the spell. *It's dangerous,* Fen had said. *And there's a catch. The person freed from the curse forgets they ever knew the person who took it.*

"I won't let you die." I gripped the little dagger tightly, pressing my forehead to the wolf's face, breathing in his wild scent. "Not for protecting me. Not for any of it."

The wolf whined softly, trying to lift his head, but he was too weak. The curse had haunted his family for generations. How many others had taken it on willingly, sacrificing everything to save another person's life?

"Now, it's my turn to save someone I love." I smiled through my tears, remembering all those times I'd longed to be wild and free, to shed the careful habits Nan had drilled into me. The ten years with Alec that had taught me to be afraid—not of what lived in the forest, but of the monster who lay down beside me in bed every night. I wasn't making a sacrifice by taking on the curse—I was claiming my freedom.

The wolf's breathing hitched, growing more ragged. No more hesitating.

I sliced my palm with the athame, barely feeling the sting. Blood welled up, dark in the shadows of the den. The looping, swirling words on the blade began to glow as I pressed my bleeding hand to the wolf's chest, feeling his heartbeat flutter beneath my touch.

"This curse I take," I whispered, the words leaping easily off my tongue. "From thee unto me."

I gulped a dry breath.

Nothing happened. I waited.

The air around us began to crackle and hum, lightly at first, the way it sometimes does before lightning strikes. My skin turned arctic cold, but everything inside me began to burn with a golden fire so intense I gasped.

The wolf's eyes widened, glowing silver-white in the darkness, his gaze locked on mine. My vision blurred, then sharpened.

Thirst. Hunger.

The wolf's heart, my heart, the drumming in our veins. The scratching of a tiny marsupial at the back of the den. Worms in the ground below. All of it so loud. The scent of blood and tears and dank earth, overwhelming—

The golden light inside me grew more intense, burning through me like wildfire, searing away everything I'd been. Everything except my love for Fen and a new, primal hunger for revenge.

The wolf's breathing steadied as my own grew rapid and harsh. He blinked up at me in confusion, already forgetting, the curse taking his memories as it left him.

I pressed a kiss between his eyes. "Goodbye, my love. It's my turn to protect you now. And I will, I promise."

Then I rose, blood dripping from between my fingers as I faced the den's entrance. My muscles trembled with new strength, my blood singing with ancient magic.

As I slipped outside, I glanced back into the den. A man lay where the wolf had been. On his side, his face resting against the packed earth, his arms before him. His skin streaked with blood, his dark hair tangled over his face. Naked, beautiful.

And no longer mine.

Outside in the darkness, I stripped out of my clothes, and threw them into the shadows, not needing them anymore. They belonged to the old me, the tame me. The me who'd been too scared to leave the path and live her life.

The me who no longer existed.

I gasped softly as moonlight touched my skin. A bright tingling coursed through me, making my blood leap and howl in my veins. The curse was stirring, unfurling the great beast that now lived deep inside me, awakening it to this new world.

It was time. Time to embrace what I'd become.

Time to hunt.

36

MAEVE

THE FOREST FLOOR sprang beneath my paws as I raced through the dawn light, following Derek's scent. My grief blazed, driving me forward, but my rage burned stronger. Once, I had feared these woods. Now, the trees and branches, the wild grasses, the vines and bushes parted before me like water, welcoming their daughter home.

A bullet whined past my ear.

He was near. I sipped the air, tasting gun oil. The dampness of sweat. And the sweet richness of my enemy's blood. I changed direction, letting the wind carry his location to me.

I found him in a weedy clearing, the stumps of all the trees he'd killed weathered back by years of rain and sun. I bounded closer, letting my mighty paws thud noisily on the hard ground.

Derek glanced up and froze, his face going slack. Then he regained himself, setting his jaw and narrowing his eyes. He aimed and fired, but all he got was the click of the pin against the breech face.

I padded closer.

Hello, Derek. My words came out as a snarl. *Months ago you threatened to eat me up—but now here I am, the big bad wolf come for you.*

Come for the man who had cut down my ancient tree, who had tormented the wolves, and killed countless other innocent creatures. Who had destroyed the only man I ever truly loved—and in the process destroyed me too.

He began to shake, his thick fingers struggling to reload as he fumbled with the cartridges, dropping them in the grass. He scrabbled for the fallen rounds, shoving them into the chamber, his voice cracking. "Get away, damn you—"

He raised the rifle, firing off a shot that struck a tree stump somewhere behind me.

I growled. The old Maeve would have shown mercy. Would have found a peaceful solution. Or given in, bowing her head to keep the peace. But that Maeve had died in the den with Fen, and this new creature had other ideas.

I stalked towards him, my massive paws now silent on the barren ground. Power thrummed through my veins—not just the curse's magic but something older. Something that remembered when humans feared the dark spaces between the trees, and with good reason.

Derek fired off another shot, but it was way off. He gave up and clutched the rifle like a club, swinging it wildly at me as he stumbled back. "Keep away, you bloody mongrel!"

I snarled softly, drawing back my lips. *Guess what, Derek? I've changed. I finally know who I am. I'm not a Lamb. And I'm not a nobody. I'm your worst nightmare.* My words were not words, but the meaning must have blazed from my eyes like a beacon.

Derek frowned, the weapon in his hands dropping just a bit as he looked at me more closely, his gaze softening.

"Maeve?"

But I was already moving. Leaping effortlessly, my muscles rippling, the snarl of revenge rumbling deep in my chest. My powerful jaws closed around his throat, and the forest drank deep.

37

MAEVE

Spring sunlight streamed through the trees as I planted another seedling in the rich earth of what had once been the sawmill yard. Native wattles and tea trees already reached toward the sky where timber had once lain stacked, and the air rang with birdsong instead of machinery.

"Mind the roots, Maeve," Nan called out, tamping down a newly planted stringybark sapling. "The soil's still thin here and they need room to breathe."

I smiled at her, grateful for her company. And her help. Six months ago, I'd have been too afraid to take on this project alone, but now the transformation of the sawmill grounds into something wild and beautiful felt like the most natural thing in the world.

Fen's tree—as I called the river red gum he'd been tied to the night of Derek's cruel bonfire—now stood in the centre of a native garden reserve. The bonfire scorchmarks were gone, but the faint rope burn around the smooth trunk remained, a reminder of how far I'd come since that night. And how much I'd lost.

"Are you done with that watering can?" Kitty asked, tromping over in her purple polka-dot gumboots, her damp face smudged with dirt under her wide-brimmed hat. "My little gum nut babies are thirsty."

I passed her the empty can and she turned to fill it at the tank, but then stopped and looked towards the road, shading her eyes.

A sleek black car rolled up the drive, its tyres crunching on gravel, its polished surface out of place in our budding wilderness.

"Brace yourself," Kitty muttered. "The queen has arrived."

Betty Lamb emerged from the back seat, immaculate as always. Her driver remained with the vehicle as she picked her way across the cleared ground toward us, her sensible heels somehow avoiding every muddy patch.

"Maeve, dear," she said, her gaze sweeping over the transformed lumber yard. "I see you've been busy."

Nan straightened, her mouth set in a grim line. There was history between these two women that ran deeper than I'd ever fully understood.

"Betty," she acknowledged, her tone sounding like a challenge.

"Posy." Betty's smile was thin. "Still digging in the dirt, I see."

"And I see you're still interfering where you're not wanted."

I stepped between them. "What brings you here, Betty?"

"Curiosity." Her narrow gaze travelled over me, then drifted to the corrugated shed that once housed the mill. "The police came to see me this morning. About Derek."

"They came here too," I said, keeping my voice neutral. "They're closing the case."

"Yes, I heard." Her gaze turned sharp. "They mentioned

you told them Derek was hunting wild dogs before he disappeared?"

"That's what he told me."

"And you think that's what happened to him?"

"I told him to leave them alone." I squared my shoulders, standing tall. Once, telling a lie would have choked me. But that was before I learned to run with the wolves, before I tasted moonlight on my tongue and the rush of the hunt. Now deception came as naturally as breathing. "I tried to warn him—after what happened to his brother—but like Alec, he never listened."

Betty nodded slowly, as though confirming something to herself. "You've gone against my wishes, Maeve. The sawmill—"

"Is mine," I finished for her. "And it's serving a better purpose now."

"As what? A garden?"

"As a sanctuary," I said. The word felt right in my mouth, powerful and true. "For all the things in this town that need protection."

Something shifted in Betty's expression—not surprise, but a kind of grim satisfaction, as though I'd confirmed a theory. "You've changed," she said softly.

I shrugged. "People do, I guess."

"Not like this." Her gaze dropped to my hands, dirt-covered and steady. "Not so quickly. So completely. As if you've become someone else entirely. I must confess, it suits you." She turned to leave, then paused, looking back, her face softening. "You remind me of her, you know."

"Who?"

"The girl I used to be." She said it so quietly I barely caught the words. "Before I learned what the forest can take from you."

I watched her car disappear down the drive, the sun glinting off the windscreen, dust swirling around the tyres.

"Good riddance," Kitty muttered.

"You're nothing like her, you know." Nan glared at the dust cloud trailing along the forest road. "She was a selfish young woman back in the day. Using others to get what she wanted, then casting them aside."

"Did you know her, Nan?"

"Well enough."

"What did she mean about learning what the forest can take from you?"

Nan dusted soil from her gardening apron and sighed. "She loved someone once, too."

I waited for her to elaborate, but instead she straightened with a groan, pressing her hands to the small of her back.

"These old bones need a rest. I'll make us some tea."

She strode towards the small shed I'd converted into a makeshift cabin, leaving Kitty and me alone among the seedlings.

"Old bones indeed," Kitty scoffed, shaking her head. "She could outwork the pair of us combined, and still not break a sweat."

I was still gazing at the road, a solitary dust plume lingering over the trees. Betty Lamb was wrong. I already understood what the forest could take. What it had taken from me. Everything. At least, everything that had truly mattered.

"Earth to Maeve?"

I glanced back. "Hmm?"

She sighed. "Go and see him."

"Who?"

"Fen."

I bent to retrieve my trowel, avoiding her eyes. Liam had told everyone that Fen got his injury from a fall onto sharp rocks while they were rescuing a kangaroo. Without the curse, Fen healed at the normal rate, and had returned to work at the animal hospital a few weeks later. That was six months ago, and I still hadn't summoned the courage to visit.

"I can't."

"Why not?" Kitty pressed. "I thought you loved him?"

"I do. It's just that..." I could still see him lying on the den floor, the confusion in the wolf's eyes as he blinked up at me, not knowing who I was. It was only an instant, but it still broke my heart all these months later. To see that same look in Fen's eyes now would crush me beyond hope. "He doesn't remember me."

"Maybe seeing you would help him remember," Kitty suggested, her voice softening. "Maybe—"

"It won't, Kit." I sighed. "You know, I've sat outside the animal hospital and watched him, trying to muster the courage to go in. But I just can't." I looked up at the sky, holding in the tears that were trying to spill down my cheeks.

Kitty patted my back.

"Hey, loser," she said gently. "I get it. You need time. And while you're waiting for your heart to mend, I'm gonna be here, okay?"

I almost told her then—about the curse, about the athame, about how the wolf now lived inside me. How sometimes I woke with dirt under my nails and the taste of the hunt in my mouth.

But then Nan returned with tea in mismatched mugs, and we sat together under the red gum tree, watching shadows stretch across the newly planted ground.

After they left, I walked to the edge of the property where the trees grew thick. A black wolf—Liam—emerged from the shadows, followed by two younger ones. They padded silently into the open area among the saplings, knowing they were safe here.

This was what the sawmill had become—a sanctuary where

the pack could hunt without fear. Where the wild things could flourish. Where I could shift beneath the full moon and run with my new family, free and fierce and finally whole.

But sometimes, on nights when the moon rode high over the hills, I caught a familiar scent on the wind. A flash of grey fur between the trees. And my heart ached with memories of soft green eyes and gentle hands and a love mighty enough to set me free.

I'll find you again, I promised silently. *In this life or the next, somehow I'll find you.*

The wolves melted back into the forest, and I returned to my garden. The seedlings would grow strong here, nourished by soil that was slowly recovering. The land around me was no longer barren but alive with possibility. Healing, and getting back to its natural state, the way it was meant to be.

Just like me.

38

MAEVE

THE FULL MOON washed the forest in silver light as I tucked my clothes beneath the old ironbark tree, my movements quick and practised after six months of surrendering to my wolf. Hunting had become an addiction, night after night, being one with the forest I once feared.

Fen had hated the curse, always at odds with its raw power. But the moment it swept out of him and into me, it felt like a homecoming. The reckless thrill I'd always craved, the freedom to be who I wished without fear. The world before me, no more paths to follow.

I didn't fear the wild anymore.

I *was* the wild.

Even in this soft human form, there was still so much of that moonlit creature in me, the half-creature that thrived in the shadows and avoided the light. The bold predator I turned into night after night.

I barely had time to inhale the damp forest air before the change rippled through me, fast and fierce. Fireflies raced through my bloodstream, tickling my bones as the curse sent minuscule shockwaves through every cell in my body. My senses became so acute that the world around me seemed to hum with possibility.

My large paws hit the dirt and I took off between the trees, bounding for the sheer joy of it. Once, being out here alone at night would have scared me.

Not now.

The dark was like a warm hug around my powerful body, bringing a thousand stories to my sensitive nose—the musty warmth of a wallaby that passed through moments ago, the sharp sweetness of nectar from the flowering gums, the zesty crackle of approaching rain. But then—*there*. Underneath it all wafted a scent that made me drool.

Rabbit.

My muscles bunched as I changed direction, falling into the rhythm of the hunt. The rabbit's scent pulsed sweet and rich, wafting through the piney woods, my blood thrumming as I closed in, my paws pounding whisper-quiet on the earth.

The rabbit scrambled left then right, its juicy heart racing, its fear-scent driving me to run faster and faster. I was so deep in chase mode that I nearly missed the growl of a motorbike engine, unable to stop as the road lurched up before me.

Headlights blinded me as I emerged onto the road, slowing too late as the overwhelming brightness glared towards me, trapping me in its mesmerising lunar blaze.

39

FEN

I SWERVED HARD, the bike fishtailing on the loose gravel as I barely missed what looked like a wild dog. The animal yelped and went down, rolling into the dark bushes on the verge. I brought the bike to a stop, killing the engine and sliding off my helmet.

I jogged back along the dirt road, fishing out my phone for light. I'd helped Liam rescue a lot of animals from the roadside, but I was madly hoping the near-collision hadn't caused much damage. I didn't even have my first aid kit with me.

I hadn't expected to ride this far, but the darkness and stars and scent of pine in the air had seduced me to keep going.

Unable to sleep. Again.

I blamed my dreams, although I never remembered them when I woke up. Just glimpses—an owl soaring through the afternoon shadows, and a green hollow filled with wildflowers. A soft voice calling my name. Part of me longed to remember, but the greater part sensed it was somehow safer to forget.

The crunch of gravel under my boots echoed in the still

night, the light beam carving through the darkness picking out a pale shape ahead of me on the verge.

"What the—?"

A woman sprawled in the leaves, her thick hair tangled around her shoulders. A very naked woman. The graze on her cheekbone was trickling blood, and she must have bitten her lip as there was blood on her chin, too.

"Jeez, you came out of nowhere." My words were gruff, like an accusation, or maybe panic, which was not like me. I knelt in front of her and spoke more softly. "You hurt?"

She blinked up at me, dazed. She must have been wearing contacts, because her eyes flared briefly in the moonlight, gleaming white-gold for a moment before turning dark again. She shook her head, her thick auburn hair spilling around her shoulders, her gaze suddenly sharp.

"Fen?"

She must know me from the clinic, though how I'd forget someone this gorgeous seemed impossible. I shrugged out of my leather coat, crouching forward to wrap it around her. "Do we know each other?"

"Of course, I—" She stopped, something flickering across her face. "I'm Maeve."

Maeve. The wind whispered through the branches, bringing the scent of wildflowers, and somewhere overhead, a boobook owl called to its mate, its mournful cry clawing at my soul.

"I'm sorry, I still don't—" I frowned. I had no memory of her, yet something about her tugged at me like a face from a dream. But how could that be?

She must be confused. A concussion, maybe. Amnesia. She had leaves in her hair and a dirt smudge above her lip—and a wild, almost joyful gleam in her eyes.

"You sure you're okay?"

Her slow smile lit up her face, as luminous as the moon. "Never felt better."

Okay, a concussion. I crouched in front of her, shining my light into her eyes, noting the enlarged pupils.

"We'll need to get you checked out."

"Trust me, Fen. I'm perfectly fine."

I blew out a long breath, wanting so badly to gather her up against me and hold her safe that a vein began to pulse in my neck. I scanned the road both ways, wondering if she'd been dumped here after a lover's spat or some crazy party dare.

"Are you sure no one hurt you? Because..." *Because if they did, I'll find the mongrels and tear them limb from limb.* "Where's your car?"

She just laughed, tilting her head back with a husky, owl-like hoot. Leaning in, she wrapped her slender fingers around my wrist and locked eyes with me.

"What brings you out at this time of night? It must be—" She glanced up at the full moon, smiling. "At least midnight. We're miles from Whitefeather Road."

Her voice was beautiful, familiar somehow. Unsettling that she knew where I lived while I couldn't place her at all. I didn't question that she knew me, though—she seemed comfortable being undressed in front of me. So why was I drawing a blank on who she was?

"We better get you back to town," I told her. "Get those scrapes looked at. That cut on your cheek might need stitching."

She touched my shoulder, her fingers drifting softly down my arm as she smiled.

"How are you with a needle and thread?"

I frowned. "I'm pretty good, to be honest. Though be warned. The last thing I stitched was a pregnant horse."

She laughed again, reaching for my hand. I helped her to her feet, trying not to notice how my coat barely covered the essentials.

"Want to tell me why you're naked in the forest at midnight?"

Her lips curved into a smile that made my pulse skip. "It's quite a story."

"I've got all the time in the world." The words came out before I could stop them, but something about her pulled at me. Like a half-remembered conversation or a song I couldn't quite place.

She padded toward my bike, bare feet silent on the road. "Give me a lift home?"

"Sure, but you'll need this." I held out my spare helmet.

She shook her head. "I like to feel the wind in my hair."

Of course you do. "It's not exactly safe—"

"Nothing ever is." She swung onto the back of my bike like she belonged there, my coat riding dangerously high. "Coming?"

I found myself grinning as I straddled the bike. Maeve's arms slid around my waist, her body warm against my back. As we rode through the moonlit forest, her long hair whipped against my face, carrying a wild scent of earth and rain and something familiar I couldn't place.

She felt dangerous, this beautiful stranger who wasn't a stranger. Like a storm about to break. My quiet life in Riverwood wasn't going to be quiet anymore, not with her in it.

Oddly enough, I didn't care.

"Go left here," she murmured against my ear, and I almost missed the turn, distracted by the way her breath tickled my neck. The road wound deeper into the forest, and I realised we were heading—not towards town, as I expected—but to my place on Whitefeather Road.

Shivers ran over my skin.

For as long as I could remember, I'd been alone, following the narrow path I laid out for myself—my vet practice and rescue shelter, and the small group of friends I hung with on weekends. Happy to tend my veggie patch and care for the wildlife Liam brought around for me to heal. Managing to ignore the loneliness that ached inside me sometimes like a broken bone.

Or heart.

But as Meave's arms tightened around me and she pressed closer, laughing into the wind, I had a feeling this wild woman was going to turn my quiet world upside down.

And God help me, I couldn't wait.

40

MAEVE

THUNDER GROWLED OVERHEAD as I pressed the last sapling into the dark soil, the old-growth forest whispering as a breeze rippled through the leaves. The ancient stump loomed behind us, its broad, weathered rings glowing pale gold in the shifting afternoon light. Our tiny new trees looked fragile against its massive base, but they were stronger than they seemed.

Like me.

A drop of rain hit my cheek. Then another. The air crackled with electricity, making the wolf beneath my skin restless.

"Storm's coming," Fen said, brushing dirt from his hands. "We should head back."

I rose slowly, the big wet dollops splashing my flushed face. This morning's blue sky had turned dark and heavy, a bank of purple clouds settling over the treetops. Below it, the forest had gone quiet, the air smelling of wet earth and pine needles.

"Not yet."

As the rain fell harder, I looked up at the rumbling sky,

spreading my arms and spinning in slow circles as my body hummed with the storm's wild energy.

Fen shook his head, laughing. "Mae, what are you—?"

I caught his hand, rain streaming down my face and plastering my clothes to my skin.

"Dance with me."

"In the rain?"

"Especially in the rain."

His eyes gleamed silvery green as he smiled, his dimples deepening. "You're crazy, you know that?"

"Crazy about you." I pulled him into my dance, both of us laughing as we whirled together beneath the storm.

Above the treetops, a pair of boobook owls cut through the deluge, their calls echoing around us. Fen saw them and stopped, something stirring in his eyes. For a moment, I wondered if he remembered—the forest, the wolf, the magic that had brought us together—but as the owls swooped into the forest and disappeared, he looked back at me, his hands finding my waist, tugging me closer.

"You realise what we're doing here, don't you?"

"What's that?" I asked, unable to keep the smile from my voice.

"We're creating history. One day our kids will come back to this place and tell stories about us."

My breath caught at the casual way he spoke of our future. "Only the good ones, I hope."

"Good, bad, the ugly. All stories are worth telling."

"Especially ours."

His arms tightened around me, his gaze searching my eyes. "Sometimes," he said, his voice rough, "I feel like I've known you forever."

You have, I wanted to tell him. *In this form and another.* Instead, I bit my lip and pressed closer, not wanting to break the spell. Rain dripped from his eyelashes, carving paths down his throat. He tangled his fingers in my wet hair, his other hand pressing against my back, pulling me tightly against him. When his lips found mine, he tasted of storms and secrets and everything wild I'd ever wanted.

Lightning flashed again, closer now. The thunder that followed shook the earth beneath our feet.

"We really should go," he whispered against my mouth.

"Why?" I wound my arms around his neck, feeling his pulse jump beneath my fingers. "Afraid of getting wet?"

His laugh rumbled through both our bodies. "Afraid of you," he said, but his hands tightened on my hips, drawing me closer. "You make me forget everything else."

I pressed my lips to his jaw, inhaling the scent of rain on his skin. Aching a little for the love story we'd lost, but grateful for this new one we were discovering together.

"As long as you still remember us, nothing else matters."

The rain fell harder now, drumming against leaves, soaking into the newly-turned earth around our saplings. Fen's shirt clung to his chest and arms, and my own sodden clothes were a second skin.

"Mae." His voice was husky as he laced his fingers with mine. "Are you happy? Here, with me?"

The old Maeve would have run from this moment. From the storm, from the wild magic singing in her blood, from the fierce joy of being held by someone who saw all of her—even the parts he couldn't remember.

But I wasn't her anymore.

I drew him into another kiss, letting my actions answer for me. His grip tightened, a growl building in his chest that was almost wolfish. Almost remembered.

But his memories would stay buried. And the magic would sleep in my veins instead of his. We had this moment, this storm, this love that refused to be tamed. We had saplings reaching for the sky and rain washing the world clean and his hands on my skin like he'd never let me go.

It was enough. It was everything.

Lightning cracked the sky open, and we danced.

ABOUT THE AUTHOR

Anna Romer is an internationally bestselling Australian author of mystery and romance, both historical and contemporary, with elements of paranormal woven in—ghosts, haunted houses, and fairytales. She's also working on a stockpile of dark romantic fantasy novels.

She lives on Australia's beautiful eastern coast, and when she's not writing she's a keen gardener, knitter, bushwalker and conservationist.

If you'd like to join Anna's newsletter for updates and deals, you can sign up at: https://annaromer.com/pages/newsletter

ALSO BY ANNA ROMER

The Outlaw's Daughter

The Ghost of Briar Rose

Lyrebird Hill

Under the Midnight Sky

Thornwood House

Beyond the Orchard